If The Slipper Fits

ELIZABETH HARBISON

SILHOUETTE *Romance*®

Published by Silhouette Books

America's Publisher of Contemporary Romance

SILHOUETTE BOOKS

ISBN 0-373-19820-5

IF THE SLIPPER FITS

Books by Elizabeth Harbison

Silhouette Romance

A Groom for Maggie #1239
Wife Without a Past #1258
Two Brothers and a Bride #1286
True Love Ranch #1323
Emma and the Earl #1410
Plain Jane Marries the Boss #1416
Annie and the Prince #1423
His Secret Heir #1528
A Pregnant Proposal #1553
Princess Takes a Holiday #1643
The Secret Princess #1713
Taming of the Two #1790
If the Slipper Fits #1820

*Cinderella Brides

Silhouette Special Edition

Drive Me Wild #1476
Midnight Cravings #1539
How To Get Your Man #1685
Diary of a Domestic
  Goddess #1727
Falling for the Boss #1747

Silhouette Books

Lone Star Country Club
Mission Creek Mother-To-Be

ELIZABETH HARBISON

has been an avid reader for as long as she can remember. After devouring the Nancy Drew and Trixie Belden series in grade school, she moved on to the suspense of Mary Stewart, Dorothy Eden and Daphne du Maurier, just to name a few. From there it was a natural progression to writing, although early efforts have been securely hidden away in the back of a closet.

After authoring three cookbooks, Elizabeth turned her hand to writing romances and hasn't looked back. Her second book for Silhouette Romance, *Wife Without a Past*, was a 1998 finalist for the Romance Writers of America's prestigious RITA® Award in the "Best Traditional Romance" category.

Elizabeth lives in Maryland with her husband, John, daughter Mary Paige, and son Jack, as well as two dogs, Bailey and Zuzu. She loves to hear from readers and you can write to her at c/o P.O. Box 1636, Germantown, MD 20875.

To Connie Atkins, the best mother, supporter, proofreader and cheerleader there ever was. Thanks, Mommy.

Prologue

Twenty-five years ago

"Easy now, climb down slowly. Slowly." Panic surged in Sister Gladys's chest as she tried to persuade the small blond toddler down from the top of the jungle gym.

The child, Lily, was always getting into things. She was fearless. Ever since she and her sisters had been left in the church adjacent to the Barrie Home for Children, it had been evident to everyone that this child was the leader of her little pack.

Sister Gladys knew that when she brought Lily and her sisters, as well as a handful of other children from the Barrie Home for Children, outside to play.

But it was such a beautiful day and they'd all been stuck inside because of rain for weeks now.

It was an impulsive decision she regretted now. Virginia Porter, the director of the home, had a rule about no more than five children per adult outdoors. Maria was out shopping and would have been back soon enough to help Sister Gladys, if only she'd waited.

But they were so eager to play. Sister Gladys had thought there would be no harm in just taking them out for a few minutes...that is, until little Dudley fell and hurt his ankle. Gladys had spent no more than one minute with her back turned to the girls and in that time mischievous Lily had climbed to the very top of the metal contraption while her sisters looked on.

"One step at a time," Sister Gladys said, taking one step up onto the jungle gym. She was terrified of heights, even low ones, so she was about the worst person for this job. But she was the only adult here. She couldn't leave, even to ask for help. It was up to her.

Lily, meanwhile, giggled, showing no signs of concern at all. Her pale golden hair glowed almost like a halo, though this child was not always an angel.

"Come on, dear." Gladys held a shaking hand out toward the child. Fortunately, Lily began climbing down. "Good girl. That's a good girl."

"Lil," a little voice called. It was Lily's more cautious sister, Rose. She frowned up at Lily, the sun bouncing off her copper hair. "Come down, Lil."

"I coming." Lily climbed confidently down the metal rungs.

"Careful," her other sister, Laurel, said. Then she became distracted by a butterfly. "Flutterby!"

Good, Sister Gladys thought, as Lily took the last step down onto the safety of the ground. The fewer witnesses, the better. If Virginia found out about this, she'd—she'd—

"Let this be a lesson to you," a voice said sharply from behind her.

Sister Gladys turned to see an angry Virginia scowling at her. "This is exactly why we have the rule requiring adult supervision for all the children when we go outdoors."

"I know. It was just such a beautiful day."

"It could have turned into a terrible day." Virginia picked up the blond child and gave her an affectionate squeeze. "Especially with this one around. You know she's always up to something." She smiled at the girl. "You have too much energy, little one." She sighed. "And way too much determination." Lily ran off as soon as Virginia put her down.

"But she's a good girl," Sister Gladys objected. "She's such a sweet little thing."

Virginia raised an eyebrow. "True, but she is as headstrong as they come. Once she decides she wants something, she won't let anything stand in her way." She shook her head and looked at the child. "It's almost uncanny how she always gets her way."

"Like when she got the cookies off the top shelf in the kitchen?"

"Exactly." Virginia smiled. "We kept telling her

no, but the minute she got her chance she went for the cookies and got them. To tell you the truth, I almost admire her for it. I just hope it doesn't get her into trouble some day."

Chapter One

"The Belvedere Suite is for Prince Conrad of Beloria. His stepmother and stepsister, Princess Drucille and Lady Ann, will be in the Wyndham Suite." Gerard Von Mises ran his fingertip down the ink-stained register of the Montclair Hotel, listing the guests that concierge Lily Tilden would be in charge of. It was old-fashioned, but that's the way Gerard, the owner of the hotel, preferred it. Computers, he said, were too impersonal.

Lily didn't tell him that she kept the records on her laptop in the office as well, just in case there was a conflict that they didn't notice on paper. Tradition was great, but a girl had to be practical as well.

"The prince and his entourage will be here tomorrow," Gerard said. "And I've arranged to have the full staff here to greet him, as his stepmother is quite... exacting about such things."

Lily nodded. She had already taken several calls on behalf of Princess Drucille. Requests were for pink towels and verbena-scented soap, and a particular brand of French spring water that Lily had paid hefty customs taxes to acquire.

"Mrs. Hillcrest leaves the Astor Suite tomorrow," Gerard continued, looking over the book. "Which leaves us with just Prince Conrad, Princess Drucille, Lady Ann, Samuel Eden and, of course, Mrs. Dorbrook for you on the executive level. The rest of their party will be on the lower floors." He sighed and turned to Lily. "It is good clientele, but business could still be better."

"Things have been tough all over the city as far as tourism goes," she assured him, though she knew the situation was serious. "It'll pick up. Especially with Prince Conrad coming. The *Post* gossip column has been positively *filled* with stuff about him."

Gerard gave a smile. "He's popular with young ladies, that much is true."

"Well, popular playboys tend to get a lot of photo ops. So you see? We'll probably get lots of business from that alone," Lily said, but she wasn't so sure. They had hosted popular celebrities before, but it usually resulted in more autograph-seekers and paparazzi hanging around outside rather than clients checking in. Still, the fact that Prince Conrad was coming would undoubtedly raise the profile of the hotel and she knew the Montclair needed that pretty desperately.

"All right." Gerard closed the book. "You've almost convinced me." He smiled. "You've worked a long day. Go home."

"You've got it." Lily had been on her feet for nearly ten hours, and it wasn't the first time this week. Since Gerard had cut the staff back, she'd had to sleep at the hotel more often than any of the guests, except for Bernice Dorbrook, who had been a resident since her oil-rich husband had died in 1983.

Now all Lily wanted to do was go home and soak in a nice hot bath, maybe with some Epsom salts thrown in. Lately there had been more long days than short ones at work, and although it was getting to her, she knew Gerard couldn't afford to hire another concierge. Between herself and Andy, they would have to handle whatever came up. "See you in the morning."

She went to the back office to collect her things. She would take a cab home tonight. She just didn't have it in her to wait for the bus and make transfers. Fortunately, Samuel Eden had given her a generous tip after she'd gotten him tickets to a sold-out Broadway show his wife had been wanting to see, so she could afford a few extra bucks to get home faster.

"Good night, Karen, Barbara," she called to the

women working the front desk. "See you tomorrow!"

Karen laughed. "It's almost tomorrow now."

"Don't remind me." Lily smiled and made her way across the rich Oriental carpet that Gerard had centered proudly on the marble lobby floor. It represented his only foray into the twenty-first century—he'd won it from an online auction after Lily had seen it there and persuaded him to bid. Even stubborn Gerard had been unable to resist the bargain.

She was about two yards from the gilded revolving door when it creaked to life and two dour-faced men walked in, wearing black suits and expressions that made her think of mobsters in old movies.

"The royal party is arriving in five minutes," one of the men said.

"Tonight?" Lily asked, glancing quizzically back at Gerard and Karen at the front desk.

Panic had frozen Gerard's features in something of a grimace. "But—but I was told Prince Conrad and his family were arriving tomorrow."

"We've had a change of plans," the other man said, his accent thick with guttural Germanic tones. He frowned. "Are you saying you cannot accommodate them?"

"Of course not!" Gerard burst. "It's just that—that we wanted to greet them properly and we are short-staffed at this hour of the night."

The men exchanged knowing glances, and Lily

imagined they were both anticipating the reaction of Princess Drucille.

"I have some requests from Her Highness." The man produced a sheet of paper from his pocket. "This is what she would like. Dinner from Le Capitan as well as some champagne and a certain kind of flower." He looked at the paper and frowned. "Birds of Paradise."

For Gerard, it probably couldn't have gotten worse. Everyone knew Le Capitan was the new hot spot in Manhattan. It was so popular that even some A-list celebrities had been turned away at the door. The food was extraordinary, but the main reason people wanted to go there was to be seen. If Lily were to ask them to deliver a meal, they would laugh at her.

However, she knew a bartender there and she was pretty sure he could put together a take-out order for her to pick up.

She sighed inwardly. So much for a hot bath and a good night's sleep. "I'll take care of this," she said to Gerard, taking the paper from him. She looked at the paper and almost laughed. *Three plain salads, no cucumbers, no dressing. Three beef filets, cooked medium, no sauce. Two triple-fudge cakes.* She could have gotten this food almost anywhere for a fraction of the cost, but royalty wanted to eat—and pay—like royalty, she supposed.

She looked at an item scribbled on the bottom of the page: *Dom Pérignon 1983, four bottles.* It was already 11:00 p.m. It wasn't going to be easy to get the champagne tonight. And the flowers? If the hospital gift shop didn't have them, she'd be out of luck.

That's what her job was about, though. Achieving the impossible for guests. And she did have a touch for it, she had to admit. Sometimes she couldn't even believe her own luck. Seat reservations would be canceled just as she was calling to ask for them; caterers would have last-minute availability. Once a famous Broadway actress had even come in from the rain just as an ambassador's assistant was asking if there was any way to win an audience with her. That coincidence had seemed nearly supernatural, but she wasn't one to look a gift horse in the mouth.

Lily was about to leave when two women, clearly mother and daughter, entered with an exaggerated air of self-importance.

"I imagined that the great Montclair would have more staff than this waiting to greet royalty," the woman said indignantly. She was almost as wide as she was tall and Lily didn't know how she managed to affect such a regal aura, but she did.

The younger, and maybe even wider, woman with her raised her chin in haughty agreement.

"We weren't expecting you until tomorrow, Your Highness," Gerard said, hurrying over to her. He gave a small, awkward bow. "Please accept my apology. I am Gerard Von Mises, the proprietor."

Princess Drucille sniffed. "Prince Conrad will be *most* displeased with this reception."

Lily could only imagine what Prince Conrad was like, given his stepmother's attitude. She hated to see poor Gerard struggling with this woman's insults, knowing that business had been so rough recently that he was lucky to have the staff he had.

"When will he be here?" Lily asked, hoping, for Gerard's sake, that he might be far enough behind to get a better showing of staff members, even if it meant pulling people off of other floors.

Princess Drucille looked as if she'd heard a fly buzzing nearby but couldn't tell exactly where it was.

"He is here now," the younger woman, Lady Ann, responded. "So you are too late."

"Tell me, boy," Princess Drucille said to Gerard, "has Lady Penelope arrived yet?"

Gerard went pale.

Lily went blank. Lady Penelope? Who was *that?*

"Lady Penelope," Princess Drucille said again, and, answering Lily's unasked question, she added, "The daughter of the Duke of Acacia. My secretary made a reservation for her as well."

Gerard snapped his fingers behind him and Karen and Barbara quickly looked in the book, but Lily knew there was no Penelope on the list, Lady or otherwise.

"She hasn't arrived," Lily said quickly. "But the Pampano Suite is ready for her." There was no Pampano Suite, but once, when a Russian dignitary had checked in at the last minute, they had configured two adjoining rooms and called it the Pampano Suite, in honor of the waiter who had come up with the idea.

Gerard looked relieved. "Of course, the Pampano Suite. Yes. I remember."

"Excellent." Princess Drucille began walking again. "Then we will retire to our rooms now and wait for our dinner. I expect it won't be too long," she added pointedly.

"Not too long, no," Gerard said. Then asked Lily quietly, "Can you do it?"

She looked at him. He was clutching his hands so tightly in front of him that his knuckles were white. His brow was drawn up as if it were being pulled by a string. "Sure," she said to him, with a little more confidence and a lot more energy than she felt. "Don't you worry about a thing."

"I don't know how you always manage these things," Karen whispered. "But if you can score dinner from Le Capitan, I will be amazed."

"Me, too. Just keep your fingers crossed for me," Lily told her.

She was about to go into the back office and start making calls when the prince himself came through the door like a cool breeze on a stagnant summer night. Lily wasn't often impressed by fame or title, but something about the man's energy, and the way he carried himself, was absolutely commanding. For a moment she couldn't take her stunned eyes off him.

He was taller than she'd realized—his broadly

muscled physique made him look more compact in photographs. Also, his eyes, even from a distance of several yards, were the most striking pale blue she had ever seen. She didn't know if that was an optical illusion because of his raven-dark hair and tanned skin, or if they really were as vivid as they seemed. He slowed as he came into the lobby and his eyes locked onto hers. For one wild moment she felt as if someone had whispered in her ear, sending shivers down her spine.

All that and a royal title, too.

No wonder women fawned over him.

Not that Lily had any intention of doing so.

"Good evening," he said, his voice clipped, and just barely accented.

"Good evening, Your Highness," she said, feeling a little silly using the unfamiliar formality.

"Ah, you know who I am."

"Of course."

His gaze was the definition of penetrating. "I'm a day early, I realize. Are my quarters ready?"

She nodded. His manners were slightly better than his stepmother's—at least he acknowledged that they might not be prepared for him. "Yes. And I'm getting ready to call Le Capitan now."

His driver came through the door carrying several heavy-looking dark suitcases and an expression of fatigue, his breath bursting out in short shots.

"Le Capitan?" the prince repeated quizzically.

"For dinner, darling," Princess Drucille said,

almost fawning but for the hard edge to her voice. "You remember."

He looked at her coolly. "I have an appointment tonight."

Her smile was false and self-conscious. "Very well."

Lily gave her very best customer-service smile. "Is there anything else we can do to make your stay more comfortable, Your Highness?"

Prince Conrad leveled his blue gaze back on her and she felt a tremor course through her. "Give me privacy," he said.

She felt taken aback by his tone and the implication that she intended to sit around and chat with him. "Of course."

He gave a short nod. "And I expect that when I have guests, you will be…discreet."

He was referring to women, obviously. Guests. Plural.

Lily had to ignore a lot with this job. This was just more of the same. Yet something about Prince Conrad's demeanor made it a little less palatable than usual. "Of course," she said again, reminding herself that any media attention he brought to the hotel would only do Gerard's business good. And she was all for anything that helped Gerard.

"Good." He turned his gaze to Stephan, who was standing at the front desk with Karen, and asked him something in his native tongue.

Stephan nodded and held up the key Karen had just handed him.

Prince Conrad gave a single nod, and both Stephan and the other man jumped to attention, picking up the suitcases and carrying them toward the elevator.

Princess Drucille watched him with a sneer, then said to Lily, "I'll be waiting for my dinner in my suite. I assume it has a dining area."

"Yes, it does, of course," Lily said, still watching Prince Conrad walk away, his trim shape and well-cut suit slicing through the atmosphere like an arrow, as Princess Drucille followed

"Lily…Le Capitan," Gerard reminded her in urgent tones, drawing her attention back. "Her Highness does not look like a woman who likes to be disappointed."

"No, she certainly doesn't. I'm tempted to go to the nearest chain restaurant and bring her a quickie salad and steak."

Karen chuckled until Gerard gave her a silencing look.

"Oh, don't worry, Gerard, I'm not going to do it. I just said I'd *like* to." Lily reached into a drawer and took out the hotel credit card. It was worn almost smooth from use. "I'll be back soon."

She stepped outside. The familiar scent of exhaust, tomato sauce and roasted chestnuts hung in the crisp November air. There was no breeze tonight, unusual in the city. It felt downright balmy. Once she started walking she found she didn't particularly want to stop. She could have just walked straight on home. It was the nature of this job, she realized, to have to occasionally work longer hours and do more legwork than she wanted to do.

Her first stop was the hospital gift shop, which had a large and costly floral arrangement that included Birds of Paradise.

Score.

Luckily, she was able to get a cab right out front and the driver waited for her while she got both the dinner and the bottles of Dom Pérignon from her friend behind the bar at Le Capitan in exchange for money and the promise of theater tickets he'd been unsuccessful in getting himself.

The deal in place, Lily returned to the hotel. To her surprise, Karen was busy at the front desk with another last-minute guest checking in—the infamous Baroness Kiki Von Elsbon.

The baroness had been to the hotel more than once, and she often appeared when there was a rumor of some eligible bachelor checked in. Last time it had been media mogul Breck Monohan. Before that, A-list movie star Hans Poirrou. Now it was Prince Conrad. It seemed no high-profile bachelor was safe from the spoiled ex-wife of the late Baron Hurst Von Elsbon.

On top of being a singularly hungry manhunter, the baroness was also one of the more unpleasant guests Lily had had to deal with in her tenure as concierge. So when she saw Kiki at the desk, she hurried down the hall to the elevator bank. She pushed the button and waited impatiently for the elevator to arrive. She took it to the second-floor kitchen to find someone to deliver the princesses' food.

"Where's Lyle?" she asked the chef. "I need him to deliver room service."

Chef Henri shrugged broadly. "He has gone home with flu. Elissa and Sean as well. And Miguel is still in Puerto Vallarta on vacation." He took his coat off the rack. "For that I have been here an extra hour myself. I'm going home."

Henri was temperamental and the recent staff shortages had made him even more so. Lily had learned a long time ago not to argue with him. In truth, she preferred it when the other chef, Miguel, was on duty.

She sighed. "Okay. Do you know where I can find a cart setup so I can take it myself?"

He gestured vaguely toward the pantry. "Elissa made some up before she left."

"Thanks," Lily said, carrying the bags of increasingly chilly food over to the cart. She stopped and looked back at Henri. "Look, I know it isn't the best method, but I have three steaks here that are getting cold. Can I stick them in the microwave to heat them up?"

Henri looked horrified. "You jest, surely!"

She shook her head. "Sorry, I'm not kidding. So, can I do it?"

He gave a dramatic sigh, then nodded. "The meat only. No more than thirty seconds." He rolled his eyes. "But I am not taking responsibility for the end result."

Lily smiled. "*Merci,* Henri. I appreciate it."

"*De rien.*" He waved his hand and headed for the exit before she could ask any more potentially offensive questions. "Good luck."

She needed it. When she got up to Princess Drucille's room, she was ushered in by a small, mouse-faced girl with worried eyes.

Princess Drucille was leaning back on the chaise lounge, talking to her daughter and another woman. "I don't care what he *wants,* he *needs* a wife, or else the entire monarchy will dissolve. And that would not suit *me* at all."

Lady Ann nodded urgently.

"So, wait," the other woman said, and Lily recognized her accent as south Jersey. "Is he or is he not engaged to this Lady Penelope?"

"Not yet," the princess said crisply. "So if you know of any eligible debutantes, I would be open to meeting them. Your paper might be very interested in having you cover this in your column."

"Search for a new princess." The woman nodded with a gleam in her eye. "I like it."

"And, at the end, he'll almost certainly propose to Lady Penelope, and I promise you will be the *first* to know. It will be a Caroline Horton exclusive."

Ah, Caroline Horton. The Page Seven gossip columnist for the *New York Tattler.*

Caroline stood and put her hand out. "You have yourself a deal, princess."

It was obvious that Princess Drucille preferred

more deference, but she accepted the woman's hand anyway. "Remember to keep our conversation confidential."

The girl who had let Lily in flashed her a nervous look, and Lily gave a silent nod and took a step back. When Caroline Horton started for the door, Lily moved back into the room as if she'd just arrived.

"Your dinner is here, Your Highness, along with the champagne and—" she gestured at the flower arrangement "—your flowers."

Princess Drucille moved to the cart, and said crisply, "One of the salads and steaks is for Prince Conrad."

Lily was confused. "It was my impression that he didn't want to be interrupted."

"Nonsense, he's expecting you. Take it to him now before it's cold." The princess made a shooing motion with her hand. "Run along."

Lily picked up the platter with the extra plate and headed for the door. It had been her distinct impression that Prince Conrad didn't want to be disturbed, but if the princess said he was expecting her, Lily was not in any position to argue.

But when she got to his room, she found the prince had company in the form of Brittany Oliver, a Hollywood It Girl from a couple of years back. It was obvious he was *not* expecting her and that, moreover, she had committed the one sin she'd so confidently told him she wouldn't: she'd invaded his privacy.

"I didn't order this," Conrad said, his voice tired, as if he'd expected just this kind of infraction from Lily.

Lily might have felt stung except that he was absolutely correct, he *hadn't* ordered it, his stepmother had. "I apologize for the interruption," she said sincerely, "but your stepmother said you were waiting for this." Out of the corner of her eye, she could see Brittany Oliver repositioning herself on the sofa so that she was more clearly in view. "She said I was to bring it to you right away."

"My late father's wife says a great many things that are best ignored." His eyes narrowed, and his jaw tightened. "This is an excellent example of one."

"I'm sorry," Lily said. "But it's my job to not ignore the wishes of our patrons, so when she said—"

"I told you I wished to have privacy."

"Yes, I realize that, but when your stepmother—"

"My late father's wife."

"—told me you wished to have dinner…. But since that is clearly incorrect, I'll take it away."

For just a moment, Lily thought she saw a spark come into his eye. "If I refuse this now, you'll have to return it to Drucille and Ann, is that right?"

Lily kept her face impassive, even though she would rather have eaten wasps than return to Princess Drucille's room tonight. "Yes."

He kept his eyes on her for another moment before taking the platter from her. His mouth curved into the slightest smile. "That will be all," he said, setting it down on the foyer table. "Thank you."

Lily nodded and was turning to leave when the actress on the sofa spoke.

"Um, excuse me? Waitress?"

Lily turned to face the woman. "What can I do for you?"

"I think there are photographers outside. Wanting to take my picture…?" She gestured airily toward the window.

Lily stood in place. "Really?"

The girl gave an exasperated sigh. "Can you look?" She gave a completely false laugh and looked at Prince Conrad. "You know how they are. Always looking for a story about me."

Lily went to the window and looked out. There was no one there. The occasional car drifting past served as the city equivalent to crickets chirping. "I don't see anyone," she said.

Brittany scrambled to her feet. "You *don't?*" She rushed in an unbecoming fashion to the window and looked out, her face falling when she saw no one. "But I told them…" She looked at Conrad. "I told my people to keep them away and I guess they did. That's good." She cleared her throat delicately and said, "Would you excuse me for a moment while I go…powder my nose?" She headed toward the bathroom, but Lily noticed she stopped for a moment to take her cell phone out of her purse.

Lily watched her go, then turned to Conrad. "Will that be all?"

He was looking in the direction of the window, and had obviously not seen Brittany take her phone. "Have there been photographers out there tonight?"

"Not that I'm aware of."

"To your knowledge has anyone on the staff made it known that I arrived early?"

"Not that I know of."

"Hmm." Again he looked in the direction of the closed bathroom door, then back at Lily. "Please hold all of my calls this evening."

"Certainly. Is there anything else?"

"No."

"All right. If you need anything, touch Zero on the telephone keypad and ask for the concierge."

"Would that be you?"

"I'm one of them."

"Then shouldn't I be able to ask for you by name?"

"Well…sure…but I might not be here. If I'm not, anyone else will be able to help you."

"Conrad!" Brittany called and she stepped gingerly from the restroom.

He glanced at her, then back at Lily and said, "Thank you."

Lily left thinking Prince Conrad looked like a man who would have better taste than to fall for a pretty but vacant starlet. On the other hand, maybe there weren't a lot of men who would take substance over appearance.

And if Prince Conrad's reputation was even half true, he was not a man who was out for substance.

She looked at her watch. It was a few minutes past midnight. She had to be back here in six hours. There was, once again, no point in going home. Especially with several staffers out with the flu.

It was to be another night in the back office. She sighed. Fortunately, the office was as comfortable, if not more so, than the rooms at the Montclair. Gerard wanted only the best, and it didn't matter if it was the best bed for a guest room, the best sofa for the office, or the best garbage can for the alley. He wanted the best, and that was what he got.

Lily stopped at a supply cabinet and took out a light blanket, then went to the office and lay heavily on the sofa. It felt good to get off her feet. Really good.

She didn't know how long she'd laid there—it felt like seconds but it might have been an hour or two—when the telephone rang. She roused herself from the sofa and went to the desk. It was an in-house call, relayed by the switchboard to the front desk. She picked it up and tried to sound as if she were awake.

"It seems there has been a security breach," said a voice she recognized as Prince Conrad's.

Lily was on alert immediately. A security breach? Had someone broken into his room? Threatened him? Her mind raced from one horrible possibility to another. "What is it?" she asked, as calmly as she could. "Should I call the police?"

"No. It's reporters. They're outside."

"Huh?" She quickly put on her professional voice. "I'll have security get rid of them."

"I don't care so much about that. What I really need is for you to find a way to get my guest out of your hotel undetected. As quickly as possible."

Lily tried to put the pieces together but was still too fuzzy-headed to manage. "I'm sorry, I don't know what you mean."

"My guest, Ms. Oliver," he said pointedly. "She needs to leave. And you need to make it happen without anyone seeing her go. Contrary to your previous assertion, there *are* photographers outside and I don't want pictures of her leaving my hotel in the papers tomorrow."

Chapter Two

"I'll be right there." Lily hung up the phone and muttered an oath. She was not in the mood for this, no matter how rich, famous, or powerful the guest was. She was *not* in the mood for it.

Lack of sleep was *really* getting to her.

She stalked to the front of the building, where a group of about five photographers with large cameras stood, looking bored or tired, smoking cigarettes and eating doughnuts.

She braced herself, then went outside. "What are you doing here?"

"We got a call that Brittany Oliver's here with Prince Conrad of La-dee-dah Land," one of them said, stubbing out his cigarette on the entry gate. "So, what's the story, they an item?"

"I have no idea who you're even talking about," Lily said. "But I do know that you're making our guests feel rather uncomfortable."

"Look, lady," another said to her, "we're just trying to do our jobs, just like you. Brittany Oliver's old news, so maybe this was all set up by her publicist, but we know Prince Conrad is in town for some UN event, and he's hot right now. So, forget Brittany Oliver. Is Prince Conrad here or isn't he?"

"I've never even heard of him," Lily responded, in a voice so sincere she almost fooled herself.

The photographer narrowed his eyes and looked at her for a moment before saying, "You've never heard of the Playboy Prince of Beloria?"

She shrugged. "Sorry."

"His father died a few weeks ago, so he's here to host some charity ball, then accept some award for his father at the UN. You've heard of the United Nations, haven't you?"

She gave a tight smile. "Vaguely."

"So the guy's pretty important in those circles. And word is, he's staying here because this is where his father used to stay, back in the days when this was a happening hotel."

"Then the word is wrong." She refused to take the bait about the hotel not being what it used to be. "But you're welcome to back off a little bit and take all the pictures you want of the place." She tried to smile, but it came off as more of a smirk. "It's really beautiful, isn't it?"

He watched her for a moment, then said to his companions, "She looks like she's on the up-and-up."

"I don't know," another one said. "If he *is* there, it's her job to tell us he's not."

Lily sighed. "Listen—like I said, you can do what you like off the property. If you publish pictures with the hotel's name, so much the better. But you *cannot* stand *here* and do it because you are making my guests uncomfortable." She smiled sweetly. "Please don't make me call the police."

"Forget it," said the lone woman in the pack. "I'm not waiting here all night to take pictures of Brittany Oliver, no matter who she's with or how many silly girls are ga-ga over him."

Several of the others began to put their equipment away.

"Thank you," Lily said to them.

"I'm not budging," one of them said. "A shot of His Royal holier-than-thou-ness is worth a hell of a lot more than a shot of the inside of my apartment."

This caused a small rumble of agreement among them. Lily knew that arguing further at this point would make her look suspicious, so she shook her head and said, "Just make sure you stay back from the property, then, or I will call the police on you for loitering."

She went back into the building trying to formulate a Plan B. By the time she got back to Prince Conrad's room, she had decided that the best place to hide a person—especially in a case like this—was right out in the open.

"How about if you put on a hat and coat, and we simply have one of the employees pick you up in his private car and drive you back to your hotel?" she suggested to Brittany.

"Aren't the photographers looking for me?" Brittany asked, in a way that made Lily think that a "no" would have been far more upsetting to the actress than a "yes."

"Yes," Lily conceded. "Which is why, when you walk right out, they won't even look at you. They'll be looking for you to be smuggled out with the laundry or some other such nonsense."

Conrad smiled for the first time since Lily had been in the room. "You're right. It's a good idea."

Lily was disarmed by his smile, and told herself it was because it was unexpected, not because he was so incredibly good-looking. "I think it will work."

Brittany glanced back and forth between the two of them. "What if one of them recognizes me?"

"Then they'll take your picture and speculate about your involvement with a man who may or may not be here," Lily said simply.

This seemed to satisfy Brittany.

At the same time, it seemed to irritate Prince Conrad—he lowered his brow and his jaw tightened a bit, but he said nothing.

"Should I call Mike to bring the car around?" Lily asked, wishing to get this exercise over with.

"Let's do it!" Brittany said, clapping her hands together. "This is going to be fun."

Fun, Lily thought wearily. This "fun" was interrupting her valuable sleep time. "Okay, I'll meet you in the lobby," she said to Brittany. "It would probably be best if you stayed in the suite, Your Highness, so you're not seen."

"I'm not used to hiding."

No, he was probably just used to hiding his dates.

"You *should* stay here, Conrad," Brittany said. "If you come out and tell them we're just friends or something, it will only fuel the fire." It may have been a trick of the light, but Brittany looked hopeful.

He looked at her curiously for a moment, then shrugged. "Whatever you wish. Thank you for coming tonight. I enjoyed our meeting and I appreciate your help."

Lily felt a little ill at this characterization of what was obviously a romantic tête-à-tête. More than that, she did not want to be here in the middle of things during their goodbye, but she was stuck.

"Me, too." Brittany threw her arms around him and kissed his cheek, while pressing herself against him in a way that made Lily feel as if she should leave them alone.

Conrad pulled away first. "Please return and let me know when Ms. Oliver is safely on her way," he said to Lily.

She sighed inwardly. Her time could be much better spent sleeping, but the guest was always the priority. "Very well," she said to him. "I'm sure it will go without a hitch."

She led Brittany down the hall and to the elevator. "We have several coats that were left behind a long time ago and never claimed," she said. "You could use one of them to cover up."

"I am *not* going to wear some stranger's smelly old coat," Brittany said haughtily. Suddenly her sweet and cooperative act was over. "No way. I've got my own coat."

"Yes, you do," Lily said, looking at the long, plush mink coat—probably real—that the actress was sporting. "I was just thinking that perhaps you would be less conspicuous in something else."

The elevator arrived and Lily pulled back the metal gates and ushered the actress on board.

"At this point, if I'm recognized, I just can't help it," Brittany said, and the look in her eyes left no doubt that she was *counting* on being recognized and photographed. "Prince Conrad and I have much more…business…to do together, so we'll just have to get used to the attention, I guess."

Lily was fairly certain Brittany would make sure of that. "Your driver is right outside the front door," she said, swallowing one or two sharp comments about Brittany's intentions. Then, to ensure that the actress wouldn't stall any longer, she added, "But I'm afraid I already see some photographers."

"Really?" Brittany turned a delighted face to the

night and Lily took the opportunity to bid her good-night and return to the hotel.

She was down to a possible five hours of sleep, and that was if she fell asleep right now. Unfortunately, she had to go back to Prince Conrad's suite first and assure him that his guest had gotten into the car safely.

She plodded back up to his suite, reminding herself with every step that this was helpful to Gerard and the hotel in general. The photographer had been right about one thing: once this *had* been a grand place, and very popular with royalty and dignitaries, yet since 2001 business had slowed down and, so far, it hadn't really picked back up.

They had done promotions, and Romantic Weekend packages, and so on, but what they needed was something to make the hotel *interesting* again. Brittany Oliver wasn't going to do that, of course, but maybe the dashing Prince Conrad could.

Lily would do everything she could to protect his privacy—she would always do her job the best she could—but that didn't stop her from sort of hoping the photographers had gotten an interesting picture or two that could show up in celebrity magazines with a caption about the location.

She figured Gerard probably hoped the same thing, but neither one of them would ever say it out loud.

When she got to Conrad's suite, and he opened the door at her knock, he looked nearly as tired as she felt.

"Has she gone?" he asked, without preamble.

"Yes, she left several minutes ago. I don't think there were any photographers there."

"Good." He met her eyes, sending shivers down her spine with his cool blue gaze. "I appreciate your discretion."

"I'm only doing my job."

"What, exactly, is your job anyway?"

She was thrown by his question. "I'm the concierge."

"Yes, you said." He nodded. "But I'm not used to the workings of such a small hotel. Does it mean, as at larger hotels, that you are charged with doing whatever is in your power to make sure your guests are comfortable and happy?"

"Within reason," she said cautiously, lifting an eyebrow in question. Something told her he was headed toward something she wasn't going to be entirely comfortable with.

"I believe, miss—" He raised a questioning brow.

"Tilden. Lily."

He looked genuinely puzzled. "Tildenlily?"

"No." She smiled. His English was flawless, but hers, she was often told, was too fast. "Lily Tilden."

"Miss Tilden," he said, as if rolling fine wine over his tongue. His voice, the low timbre, the faint accent, was magnetic. It was the voice of a hypnotist. "I'm afraid you may be in for some trouble, Miss Tilden."

She swallowed hard. She was embarrassed to

admit, even to herself, that this man made her feel nervous. Lily *never* got nervous. "Oh? How so?"

"My father's wife can be—how do I say it?—demanding. You will get little rest while she's here, I'm afraid. I'd like to offer you my apologies up front."

"Well," Lily wasn't sure how to respond, "thanks for the warning. I guess. But I can handle it."

"Indeed." He gave a shrug, as if to say *I warned you*. "Good luck, Ms. Tilden."

She smiled. "Sounds as if you think I'll need it."

He smiled back, a dazzling movie-star smile. "Where my father's wife is concerned, we *all* need some luck."

Lily started to go, then stopped and turned back. "I don't mean to be impertinent—"

He raised an eyebrow and looked so amused that she nearly lost her train of thought. "Please do."

She went on, a little disconcerted, "Well, Princess Drucille spoke with great authority when she said you were expecting me to bring your dinner to you, but apparently she was…incorrect."

He nodded, and continued to look amused as Lily ran the risk of hanging herself.

"My question is this—if, in the future, she should give any of the staff instructions where you're concerned, should we assume…" She paused, unable to come up with a nice way of saying "She's not to be taken seriously" or "She's full of it."

"If I require something, I'll ask for it directly," Conrad supplied, finally letting Lily off the hook.

"Otherwise…" He shook his head. "Don't take another's word for it."

Her shoulders sagged in relief at his comprehension. "Good. I'll let the staff know."

He nodded solemnly. "I'd appreciate it. If someone arrives at my door every time Drucille wants to use my name, I'll never get any peace."

Chapter Three

To the surprise of no one, especially Lily, all of the late edition papers carried a mention of Brittany Oliver and Prince Conrad the next afternoon. There were photos as well, but none clear enough to identify the hotel. Lily had decided not to point it out to Gerard, but it didn't matter, he saw it himself.

"It would have been nice," he said, closing the paper and setting it aside. He sighed and raked a hand through his thick gray hair. "I don't know how much longer we're going to be in business if things don't get better soon."

Lily's heart ached to see this man she cared for feeling so down. Gerard Von Mises had worked hard all his life. In all the years Lily had known him, he had never missed a day at work. Yet now it was beginning to feel as if it was all for nothing, and she hated to see how despondent he looked.

"Things will pick up," she said, as she'd said hundreds of times before. But she, like Gerard, was losing faith.

It wasn't for herself that she was concerned. She could get a job almost anywhere, and had often toyed with the idea of living overseas, in Europe or Japan.

But this was Gerard's life, and he'd put his whole heart into it. Every detail of the hotel had his fingerprint on it, and Lily couldn't bear the idea of that disappearing.

"I'm sure they will," Gerard said, effectively closing the book on the conversation. "It will be all right. It always has in the past."

Lily glanced at the register, and at the number of empty rooms, and simply said, "Yes."

The phone at the concierge desk rang and Lily said, "Excuse me. Duty calls."

"That's what I like to hear," Gerard said.

She smiled and picked up the receiver. It was Stephan, Prince Conrad's bodyguard, calling to inquire about security on the perimeters of the property. Lily detailed property boundaries for him, and explained the law as far as trespassing on private property versus standing on public property. With a little prodding, Lily learned that it was not Prince Conrad who was concerned so much as Stephan himself, as he was head of the prince's security.

The prince, it turned out, did not like to have any security at all, but it was in deference to his late father's wishes that he brought the token team of two along with him. But Stephan had worked for Prince Frederick as well, and agreed with the late prince that there should be much stronger security around a royal.

After trying to reassure him that the hotel itself was quite secure, Lily ended up giving him the name of a local security company, where he could hire additional guards if he saw fit. Personally, she didn't like the idea of a whole lot of security personnel stationed about the hotel, but it was not her place to tell a guest that their security wasn't important enough to mar the environment.

When she'd finished with that call, there were three more in rapid succession; Lady Ann, who had a list of snack foods she wanted picked up from the local market; Kiki Von Elsborn, who needed the name of the general manager of Melborn's department store because a salesman there had "unfairly" accused her of shoplifting when she "accidentally" wore two pashmina shawls out of the store; and Portia Miletto, a wealthy young Italian who had left her PDA—and all of her private information—in a cab and needed Lily to track it down.

That took most of the afternoon.

When Lily finally got back from the tailor shop of the man who had found the PDA, she was fifty reward dollars lighter and several hours more exhausted.

Yet when the call came from Prince Conrad's suite that he wanted to have a moment with her, her adrenaline surged and reanimated her.

She went upstairs and knocked on his door.

He opened it after a few moments and said, "Lily. Thank you for coming."

"It's not a problem. What can I do for you?"

He looked at her for a moment, his handsome face still. Then he frowned slightly and said, "Could you come in for a moment and join me for a drink?"

Lily was taken aback. She was used to delicately avoiding the advances of male guests at the hotel… but then again, she was used to those male guests being a lot older and a lot less attractive than Prince Conrad.

He must have sensed her hesitation because he added, "I require your help with something."

"All right," she said. "Anything I can do to help."

"Please. Come in." He led her into the sitting room, which of course she knew as well as the back of her hand. "Have a seat."

She sat on the sofa.

He poured a glass of champagne and held it up to offer it to her, but she shook her head. "On duty," she explained.

"Ah." He smiled and set the glass down, instead taking out two of the pricey mineral waters Princess Drucille had ordered. He opened one for Lily and handed it to her. "Most women don't turn down champagne."

"I'm sure there are a lot of things women don't turn down when you offer it to them."

He smiled and studied her for a moment, before he said, "You don't have any undue respect for my position, do you Ms. Tilden?"

"I respect all of our guests equally."

He laughed out loud. "Good answer. Your candor is quite refreshing."

Despite herself, she flushed under his praise. "So what was it you needed my help with?"

He sobered immediately. "It's a little…awkward," he began. "We spoke of discretion last night and this is a matter that needs a great deal of it."

Lily shifted her weight in her seat, suddenly fearing the worst. Had he killed someone? Did he need help disposing of the body? Just how far did her job loyalty extend? "What is it?"

"Brittany Oliver."

There it was. He hadn't killed someone. She almost wished he had—it would have been easier than dealing with Brittany Oliver. "Yes?"

"Well, she's…I believe she may be—" he paused "—*determined* when it comes to seeing me again. In other words, I think she may come back to the hotel."

Lily wasn't quite sure what to say. On the one hand, she was quite sure he was right and, moreover, she was quite sure Brittany Oliver could become a huge pain in her backside over the next week. But on the other hand, Lily was a little put off by the fact that Prince Conrad, who had spent quite a bit of time with Brittany in his private suite doing heaven-knew-what last night, was now evidently trying to scrape her off completely.

It was hard to respect that.

"What is it you're asking me to do?" Lily asked.

"I'm asking if you could help run interference for me, as you say. Should Ms. Oliver call or come by, I'd like for you to tell her that I am not in."

This was ugly, Lily thought. But it wasn't outside the realm of her job description, as long as she didn't have to get personally involved. "In other words, you want a *do not disturb* placed on your suite."

"Yes, where Ms. Oliver is concerned."

Irritation pricked at her conscience. "Your Highness, it's common procedure to hold calls, but it's not as common to screen them. Perhaps what you need is to hire a private secretary to handle your administrative needs."

"My private secretary did not accompany me on this trip and I cannot trust just anyone with my private affairs. That's why I'm asking for your help— because I'm already in a position of having to trust you."

"I'm not sure I'm comfortable with this."

"Do you have to be?"

Her annoyance grew. "Your Highness, with all due respect, my job description does not include eliminating unwanted affections for clients, no matter who they are."

He looked amused. "And if the person in question

were a man rather than a woman…what would you do if I asked you to block the phone calls of a particularly persistent reporter?"

He had her. That would be exactly the kind of thing Lily would take on, and with gusto.

"That would be different."

"Really?"

"Of course."

"How?"

He was really putting her on the spot. "Well," Lily stalled, "for one thing, that would be an invasion of privacy for a guest. That's the sort of thing we *do* try to prevent."

"And what's to say Ms. Oliver's advances aren't an invasion of privacy?"

"Your date with her last night, for one thing," Lily said, and immediately regretted saying it.

Fortunately for her, Prince Conrad didn't take the sort of offense he could have. Instead he just raised an eyebrow. "Date?"

"Isn't that what you'd call it in your country?"

"No." The look he gave her was challenging.

Lily shrugged. "It's not my business either way—"

"No, it's not."

"But speaking as a woman, I just have a really hard time trying to fend this poor girl off for you after you spent the evening with her last night."

He smiled, but not patiently. "I'd hardly say we 'spent the evening together,' Ms. Tilden."

"And it's not my business anyway—"

"No, it's not."

"But I'm just not comfortable being asked to lie to someone on anyone's behalf."

He looked at her for a long, icy moment.

"Is it a lie," he began at last, "if you tell my female callers that I am unavailable and you take a message?"

All female callers. That was different. Sort of.

Lily sighed. "I'll do what I can."

He nodded, as if this met his approval. "Very good. I'm sure you'll do just fine."

She hesitated, then asked, "Are you like this with all of your girlfriends when you lose interest in them?"

He gave a short spike of laughter. "Are you like this with all of your guests?"

After a long moment, she said, "It depends on the circumstances, I suppose."

"Ah. It is the same with me."

It seemed like no matter what she said, he had her. "Touché," she said. "You win. I'll do what I can." She stood to leave, but he stopped her.

"I have a question, Ms. Tilden."

"Yes?"

"Are you this difficult with all of your guests' requests?"

She smiled. "No. I just don't like to help in making other people feel bad, or rejected."

He considered this for a moment, then nodded. "That's probably an admirable trait."

"Thank you. Will there be anything else?"

"No."

"All right, then. Don't hesitate to call if you need anything." She trotted out the familiar phrase, then left the room, as annoyed with herself as she was with him. What was wrong with her? She'd been asked to do ridiculous things in the name of her work before, and it had never troubled her on this level. This wasn't even that big a deal. Why was it that this time she found the idea of screening calls and visitors so distasteful? It wasn't as if she were a Brittany Oliver fan or anything.

Her feelings, upon being asked to field the calls, were way too personal and that was crazy.

As she went back down to the office, she told herself that she was offended, not as a hotel employee, but as a woman. She didn't like partaking in deceit against this woman just for this man's convenience, now that he was finished with her.

Though again, truth be told, she was almost a hundred percent sure that Brittany had committed the bigger deceit in arranging to have the photographers show up.

And Lily's having to deal with the photographers had taken more of her time than a little visitor screening would...

No, she told herself, it was still wrong for him to ask her to do that. That was all there was to it.

The next morning was filled with requests from the royal party and their entourage, from spa treatments and private fashion shows for Princess Drucille and Lady Ann to special meals delivered to Stephan and the other security guard, because they could not leave their charges.

As if that wasn't enough, there were also many requests from Baroness Kiki Von Elsbon, who was trying her subtle best to find out who was in the hotel and where, exactly, he might be staying. And eating. And going when he left the hotel. Her ploys were so transparent that they might have been amusing if Lily wasn't so frantic trying to keep up with everyone's needs.

Later that afternoon, she went to check on longtime resident Bernice Dorbrook, who was always a pleasure to spend time with. Bernice was what some would have called "a pistol." A straight-shooting Midwestern woman who had, long ago, married well—several times over—and enjoyed the company of some of the most famous people in recent history. Her stories about Cary Grant and Myrna Loy and Jack Benny and so on were always a pleasure to listen to. And one thing Bernice enjoyed more than anything else was a good, long gossip session.

"I understand we have royalty staying with us this week," Bernice said, letting Lily in her suite and closing the door behind her. "Prince Conrad of Beloria? Tell me everything."

Chapter Four

Lily smiled patiently. "Yes, you've heard right. His Highness is upstairs."

"Oooh!" Bernice clapped her hands together. "Looks like you find him intriguing! Tell me everything you know!"

"Mrs. Dorbrook," Lily began, smiling at the older woman's enthusiasm. "I am *not* intrigued by Prince Conrad."

Bernice Dorbrook raised an eyebrow and studied Lily. "I've known you for five years now, my dear. I've never seen you outwardly exasperated with anyone. Prince Conrad has been here not twenty-four hours and he's already gotten your goat." She winked broadly. "That's intriguing in *my* book."

Good lord, she was right. Lily was almost never reactionary with people, especially with hotel guests. What was it about Prince Conrad that got her going like this? It was absolutely insane. And, frankly, it was happening at the worst time possible, since she needed to help Gerard, and Gerard regarded Prince Conrad's visit as, potentially, a great boon to business.

"Is he as good-looking as he is in his pictures?" Bernice asked eagerly. "Tall, dark and handsome?"

"He's—" There was no denying it. He was the absolute *definition* of tall, dark and handsome. "He's attractive in a sort of tall, dark, European royalty sort of way."

"But those eyes," Bernice said, then made a dramatic show of sighing. "As blue as Paul Newman's."

Lily smiled and said, "Maybe. Almost. But, believe me, he's an arrogant sonofagun, too."

"Mmm, just how I like 'em." Bernice smiled and wiggled her eyebrows. "And I happen to know, I'm not the only one who feels that way."

Lily smiled. "No, probably not."

"I knew his father many years back, you know."

"No, I didn't know." Now Lily was interested. "What was he like?"

"He was just a wonderful man. Not as good-looking as his son—" she paused to chuckle "—not by a long shot, actually, but so good-hearted that you didn't even notice. He cared about everyone, especially the underprivileged. It was really quite inspiring."

Lily was suddenly fascinated. "Did you know his wife, too?"

"Barely." Bernice shook her head sadly. "She was a very quiet woman, supported her husband, loved her child, but almost never spoke in public. I always felt maybe she was sickly. I believe it was rheumatic fever as a child. Her heart was weak her whole adult life. When she passed away, I'm sorry to say I wasn't all that surprised."

"Oh, that's so sad." Lily clicked her tongue against her teeth. "I have a feeling her son could have benefited from having his mother around longer. He might have had more respect for women."

Bernice narrowed her eyes and studied Lily for a moment, before saying, "So he's giving you a lot of trouble, is he, sweetie?"

"Tons."

"Hmm."

Lily frowned at her friend, though she'd known the woman long enough to know exactly what she was getting at. She'd also known her long enough to joke with her about it. "What do you mean, hmm? Are you implying something?"

"Me?" Bernice put a hand to her chest and feigned surprise. "Why, no, my dear." She shook her head. "I'm only making a…well, a very small observation."

Lily narrowed her eyes skeptically. "And what observation is that, exactly?"

Mrs. Dorbrook shrugged dramatically. "That you would make a *lovely* princess."

If Lily had been drinking from a glass of water at that moment, she would have done a spit-take worthy of Danny Thomas. "A lovely what?"

"You heard me, a lovely *princess*." Bernice lowered her chin and looked at Lily pointedly. "As in *Princess Lily of Beloria*."

Lily gave a bark of laughter. "Oh, come on. Trust me, you don't want to be making any wagers on that. As long as I don't end up in jail as a murderess at the end of this week I'll be satisfied."

"See?" Bernice pointed a finger at her. "That's how I know. I never married a man I didn't want to kill first. That's how you know you've got a truly passionate relationship."

"Oh, Bernice." Lily went to the woman and put a hand on her shoulder. She gave a gentle squeeze. "You are such a hoot. But believe me, in this particular case, there won't be any killing *or* any marrying. In all seriousness, I'll just be glad when the guy has checked out of the hotel for good."

"We'll see," Bernice said airily. "Meantime, keep me posted on his doings. I just *love* gossip about royalty."

"Unfortunately, you're not the only one," Lily said, and told her about the photographers who had camped outside trying to get pictures of Brittany Oliver and Prince Conrad. "I have a bad feeling

Brittany Oliver isn't going to be the only would-be princess hanging around here."

"Perhaps not," Bernice agreed, then sobered noticeably and leaned forward to add, "You have bigger fish to fry."

Lily was surprised. "What, you mean Prince Conrad?"

"No." Bernice gave her a pointed look. "I mean Princess Drucille. Or—" she paused, as if waiting for a drum roll "—Drucille Germorenko, as she was known in my day."

Lily drew in a breath, genuinely surprised at this revelation. "You *know* her?"

"Only vaguely." Bernice waved her hand. "But enough to know she was a bullheaded woman, even fifty years ago. She's got a queen complex if there ever was one, and I do *not* confuse that with a princess complex. If I remember her correctly being a princess isn't quite good enough for Drucille Germorenko."

Lily couldn't help being swept into Bernice's dramatic storytelling. "No?"

Bernice shook her head. "Watch out for that one. Take my word for it, you do *not* want to get in the way of Drucille Germorenko."

The next day, Lily began to get a real inkling of what Bernice meant about Prince Conrad's difficult stepmother.

Her day had begun with a request from Princess Drucille to contact a very popular hairstylist and get him to come to the hotel and coif the princess and her daughter. Price, the princess said, was no object, and it was only that phrase that finally got Francois Labeaux, through his assistant, to agree.

No sooner had Lily achieved that minor miracle than another call came from the princess's suite, this time asking that a second maid be sent up to clean the single spot of dirt the first maid had "carelessly" left behind on the doorknob.

There was no telling how Drucille had managed to find that spot, but Lily suspected she had been looking for it.

And so it went. Every time there was a problem in the princess's suite, it seemed that Lily was the one to get the call. When, late in the afternoon, she was told she had yet another royal request, she was half-ready to have them tell the princess she had already left for the day.

But it wasn't the princess on the line when Lily picked up. It was Prince Conrad.

"Please come to my room."

"What is it?" she asked.

"It's somewhat sensitive," he said. "I need to speak with you in private."

She paused, wary of his tone, then said, "Okay, I'll be up in a moment."

As she passed the lobby, she saw that a horse-faced woman who could only have been Lady Penelope, was checking in. When she heard the woman's upper-crust British accent, she was certain it could only belong to the daughter of a duke.

So that was who Princess Drucille had in mind for Prince Conrad, Lily mused.

It was an odd pairing at best. Now, Lady Penelope might have the most wonderful personality in the world, but even so, Lily's gut instinct told her that this wasn't a woman Prince Conrad would ever be interested in. Whether it was looks or vibe or what, Lily couldn't say what she based her assessment on.

But she was sure she was right.

Lily passed the front desk without comment and got into the elevator still thinking about the conversations she'd heard between Drucille and the newspaper columnist. What was Conrad's stepmother up to? And from whom was it meant to be kept, if she was talking about having it printed in some sort of newspaper?

Lily was amazed at the number of secrets she was already having to keep for just these two hotel guests. Of course, it *was* part of the job. And she had, on very rare occasions, had to cater to estranged husbands and wives without letting them know the other was checked in to a room down the hall.

Nevertheless, this was different. This was… harder, somehow.

She knocked on Prince Conrad's door and he opened it almost immediately. He didn't greet her, but instead pulled something small out of his pocket and said, "This was in the chandelier."

"What is it?"

He dropped it onto the coffee table, and it clattered like a small marble, then rolled onto the floor. "It's a microphone," he said. "What you'd call a *bug*."

"A *bug?*" she repeated incredulously. "A recording device?" This was unbelievable.

"Exactly."

This wasn't computing. "Someone bugged the room?"

He turned to her sharply. "You're unaware of this?"

"Of course I'm unaware of it. Why would anyone want to bug your room?"

"That was what I hoped you could tell me."

"I can't even imagine."

He nodded. "That is what I thought you'd say, unfortunately."

Lily's astonishment turned to suspicion. He wasn't asking her *if* she knew something, he was asking her *what* she knew.

It was a whole different intention.

"What are you suggesting?" she asked him cautiously.

"That someone has put a microphone in my suite in this supposedly secure hotel, leading me to the obvious conclusion that it is *not* a secure hotel."

"This *is* a secure hotel."

"Yet clearly someone inside the premises is responsible for this." He looked at her evenly, but did not look away.

Lily took his meaning immediately. "Is there someone in particular you have in mind when you say that?"

He raised an eyebrow. "Two nights ago, shortly after you came to my room and saw Ms. Oliver, photographers were notified that she was here."

"That's right, but we already—"

"Today, that amateurish piece of espionage equipment fell out of the chandelier and into my breakfast." His voice was hard, but controlled. "I might have believed the photographers were a publicity stunt set up by Ms. Oliver, but this—no one had access to my room except myself and the hotel staff."

And Ms. Oliver, Lily thought, but she kept it to herself. She couldn't accuse Brittany Oliver just to deflect blame from herself and she certainly had no proof that Brittany Oliver had anything to do with this. What would she have to gain from it?

"So?" Conrad asked.

"So what? What are you asking me?"

He looked impatient. "I am asking, do you have a reasonable explanation for any of this?"

"I—" She stopped. She could concoct explanations all day, but they would only be guesses. She had no proof of anything. And, although any fool could have seen right through Brittany Oliver's terrible acting job, Lily couldn't say she'd gone so far as to bug the room.

Why would she?

For that matter, why would *anyone*? Who would have an interest in doing that? A reporter, maybe.

Caroline Horton? But again, she couldn't say that conversation she'd overheard in Princess Drucille's suite was definitely linked to this.

As a matter of fact, she couldn't say *anything* about the conversation she'd overheard, because it was her job to be discreet, to not repeat things that she heard in the privacy of people's rooms.

No matter what she overheard.

So she had to keep all of her suspicions to herself, even at the risk of incriminating herself.

"You what?" the prince demanded, his blue eyes flashing like flint.

"I'm sorry, but, no, I don't have an explanation," she said simply, trying to squelch her own pique. That was not her place, she reminded herself.

And now, when Gerard was more worried than he'd ever been about the future of his business, was not the time for her to make waves with his most prominent guests.

"I have no idea how it got here," she finished lamely.

Conrad shook his head. "Then at best you have security problems here."

Lily straightened. "And at worst?"

He looked at her. "At worst, someone here is dishonest."

It was easy to take it personally, even though, she was able to admit to herself later, he hadn't actually accused her, personally, of anything. Still, he'd gotten her dander up. "Listen, Your Highness, you may occupy a grand station in your country, and admittedly you are a guest in my hotel, but you do *not* have the right to talk to me that way."

"Then perhaps I should speak with your employer."

She shrugged. "Feel free. But I doubt he will have an explanation for you, either. We can boost security for you, and we can send a specialist up to sweep for other bugs if it would make you feel better. For that matter, I could give you an accounting of where I have spent every moment since you checked into this hotel. It shouldn't be too difficult, considering that virtually all of my time has been spent accommodating your family and friends."

He watched her, his arms folded in front of his chest, waiting for her to finish.

"But if you're really concerned about your privacy and maintaining some measure of anonymity," Lily went on, "I suggest that you be very careful about the company you keep."

"What are you implying?"

She splayed her arms. "Nothing at all."

He narrowed his eyes at her. "You, Ms. Tilden, are extremely brazen."

"Not usually. Now if you'll excuse me, I do have other guests to attend to."

She didn't wait for his answer. She simply turned on her heel and marched out of the room, and straight down to Gerard's office to tell him what happened so he could fire her from the best job she'd ever had.

Chapter Five

Conrad watched Lily go, with mingled feelings of irritation and admiration. In the end, though, it was the admiration that won out. He hadn't spent a lot of time in America, so perhaps this was what was to be expected from American women, but he had never met a woman who so willingly flew in the face of his authority.

As a matter of fact, Lily Tilden didn't have any regard for his authority whatsoever.

It was…interesting. Frustrating, certainly, and there was the potential for it to become a problem, but so far it was more amusing than anything else. He didn't have any intention of speaking to her employer about her, at least not in any negative sense. Why, if the proprietor of the Montclair was half as sycophantic as the hoteliers in Europe, he'd fire her on the spot and she didn't deserve that.

As a matter of fact, he'd like to hire her himself, if only to mill around his office and occasionally remind him not to take himself too seriously.

Smiling at the thought, he stood and walked to the window of his suite, looking out at the busy street below.

New York was a powerful place, full of life and history. Once he had thrived on city life, but lately he found he missed the more quiet towns of Beloria. Especially now, as the Christmas season approached, he missed the verdant smell of live evergreens that surrounded the palace, and the gingerbread rows of shops, almost always covered in an icing of snow from November to April.

When he was younger, he hadn't appreciated the beauty of his homeland. Instead he had appreciated the ski resorts and the snow bunnies who had come from around the world to enjoy the excellent skiing of Beloria. His father's passionate proclamations about the wonders of Beloria had fallen on deaf ears, though he could hear the echoes of them still. And now he knew how important it was.

Conrad had never felt particularly passionate about anything in his life, but he'd respected his father tremendously and he wanted to honor his memory. The best way for him to do that was to do his best to be a fair and honest head of state, a position that amounted to little more than a figurehead, and to do the best he could to call attention to his father's charitable foundation.

And it had to be the right kind of attention. No more "playboy prince" stories for him. He had to be smart about getting attention while at the same time keeping it from becoming *negative* attention.

There was no room in that plan for people like Brittany Oliver. Once he would have found her attractive enough, though that type was wearing thin for him, but now he knew he had to be a lot more careful about who he was seen with and what people made of it. Brittany clearly wanted publicity for herself, which meant she was apt to try and whip up a scandal and tie it to herself and Conrad.

He couldn't afford that, which was why he'd asked Lily Tilden to try and help keep Brittany at bay.

But still, Brittany's basic idea was sound, he had to admit it. Nothing was more interesting to the newspapers and magazines than a romance. It had always been so. Now for her part, she wanted to use that publicity to create interest in her career, but Conrad could use the same publicity to create interest in his father's works.

He would have preferred another way, of course, but he was limited. Conrad knew that the primary things that interested people in him were his age, marital status and his title. So he could talk until he was blue in the face about his father's charity, but unless he was standing beside someone the media could speculate as being "the future princess of Beloria," he wasn't going to get that much attention.

He sighed and turned away from the window, facing the neatly austere sitting room that was to be his base of operations for the next few days. It was funny how familiar the place felt; it might have been decorated by the same person who had decorated the palace of Beloria two hundred years ago. The furniture and walls were dark wood with muted colors and the walls were decorated with old-fashioned oil landscapes.

It was both comfortable and disconcerting at the same time.

He went to the wet bar and took out a cold mineral water. He twisted the top off and threw it into the trash can across the room. It made it. He smiled at the small pleasure.

But his smile faded as he turned his thoughts back to the purpose and gravity of his mission here in New York. He had to concoct a plan to make the most of his time here.

And as he sipped the cold water, a plan began to come to him.

If the media wanted to know about his romantic life, he'd give them something to sink their teeth into…just a little. He needed to create the *appearance* of a light—but not scandalous—romance that would bring the spotlight to him, and then he could turn that spotlight on the charity.

But what woman could fill the role?

Clearly Brittany Oliver was out. For one thing, she wasn't capable of the sort of acting that would be necessary to pull this off. For another thing, she was far too interested in being notorious. She didn't care how negative the publicity was, as long as she looked good in the photos and they spelled her name correctly.

No, what he needed was someone attractive, but understated. Someone who had no personal agenda as far as publicity went. Someone who was used to dealing with the media and who would remain calm and cool in a stressful situation.

What he needed was someone like Lily Tilden.

Over the next couple of days, Lily noticed a few odd things about what was happening with the royal party.

Princess Drucille and Lady Ann appeared to be doing everything within their power to put Lady Penelope in Conrad's path.

When Conrad's car showed up on the street in front of the hotel, inevitably Lady Penelope showed up in the lobby, looking rather lost and forlorn until Conrad appeared, whereupon she would pounce on him in an awkward, gawky way, asking directions to famous museums and so on. Each time, he carefully disentangled himself from her, suggesting she speak with Lily or Andy or Karen; or, better still, get into a cab and tell the driver where she wanted to go.

Each time she approached him, she was roundly shot down, yet she continued to show up, almost like a nervous kid being pushed on stage by an overbearing stage mother.

When Conrad ordered room service one evening, Princess Drucille had managed to convince the poor, unwitting waiter that Conrad was joining herself, Lady Ann and Lady Penelope in *her* suite, so he delivered the meal there. When Conrad called to inquire as to what was taking so long, he was told by the poor kid that his stepmother had headed him off in the hall and instructed him to take it down to her suite instead.

That little trick had almost gotten the waiter fired, except that Lily stepped in and explained to Conrad that he was new and hadn't been informed of Princess Drucille's heavy hand.

It wasn't until Conrad informed her that Lady Penelope had shown up, along with Princess Drucille and Lady Ann, at the restaurant where he had booked lunch with some of his foundation's U.S. officers, that Lily started to realize what might be going on.

Every time Lady Penelope and company showed up where Prince Conrad was supposed to be, it was after he made a call from, or had a conversation in, his suite.

Though it was early in the morning when it occurred to her, Lily marched up to his suite and knocked soundly on the door until he answered it.

"Is this a fire drill?" he asked, rubbing his eyes.

"Worse, I'm afraid," she said. She produced a key from her pocket and whispered, "Can you come with me for a moment?"

"Where to?" he asked, though he was already with her.

She put a finger to her lips and led him down the hall to a vacant room at the opposite end. Glancing right and left, she opened the door and ushered him in.

"I have to say, Ms. Tilden, I didn't think you were so forward."

For a moment, she was alarmed, but when she looked at him, she could see he was kidding. "Very funny."

"Well, tell me, what are we doing here?"

"I have some rather disturbing news for you," Lily began carefully. "And I realize that telling you this could lose me my job, but, on the other hand, *not* telling you could lose me or someone else here our job as well, so I'm just going to dive right in."

Conrad looked thoroughly confused. "Okay…?"

She took a breath and paced the floor in front of him. "Okay. Here goes. Do you remember the other day when you found the microphone in your room?"

He pursed his lips and tapped his finger against his chin in mock thought. "Hmm….I believe I do."

"All right, all right, of course you do." She took a quick, stabilizing breath. "I think I've figured out what's going on."

"You think my father's wife is behind it."

"I think Princess Drucille and Lady Ann might have something to do with—" She stopped. "What did you say?"

He nodded. "Every time I call for a car or ask for a reservation, they show up."

"Yes." Lily nodded eagerly. "So you think it's them, too?"

"Absolutely."

It was a tremendous relief to hear him agree. There had been a real risk in telling him she suspected his family was spying on him, but it had to be done. "We have to have the room swept right away," Lily said. "I know a guy who used to be with the—"

"It's already done," Conrad said.

"It *is?*" Her jaw dropped. "When?"

Conrad yawned. "Last night. I had someone in after the shrews went to sleep."

"Oh." Okay, now suddenly she'd gone from feeling like the clever heroine to the last horse in a race. "Good. That's good."

Conrad nodded. "So thank you for your concern but I'd really like to get back to sleep. I had a late night."

Lily had left while he was out and now she felt even more foolish wondering where he'd been and with whom. "Of course." She swallowed her embarrassment. "I'm so sorry to have troubled you."

He opened the door and started trudging back down the hall, with Lily behind him. "It was no trouble at all. Good work, Ms. Tilden. You did a good job."

"So did you."

He stopped and turned to look at her, a rakish smile on his unshaven face. "We'd make a good detective team, like something from 1970s television. Conrad and Lily."

She shrugged. "Or Lily and Conrad."

His smile broadened. "You are one feisty young woman. I have to say, I don't meet many like you."

"You're probably glad of that."

He considered that for a moment, then nodded. "Actually, I think I am."

She barely had a moment to feel bad before he continued.

"But I'm quite happy to have met the one."

The one. For one insane second—no, a fraction of a second—those words sent Lily's heart tripping.

That was weird.

She hurried to cover up any reaction he might have perceived. "For what it's worth, I'm glad to have met the only stubborn, brash crown prince I'm likely to meet."

He laughed out loud. "Don't be too sure of that. We're everywhere. *You* are far more unique than I."

Again, her heart tripped.

Again, she felt impatient with herself for reacting that way.

"Well, here's your room," she said, indicating the door they were approaching. "Sorry to have woken you for nothing."

"To the contrary, Ms. Tilden. I actually quite enjoyed myself with you." He gave a slight bow.

"Please feel free to wake me any time. I've woken to much more troubling sights than you."

She didn't dare ask what he meant by that. It was easy enough to imagine. Instead she gave a brief smile and said, "Let me know if you have any more trouble. I do have a connection who is very good at taking care of this kind of security matter, although it sounds like you've already got that covered."

He gave a single nod. "I hope so. In my position, though, one never knows. In fact, maybe I ought to have your friend come in and double check."

"I'd be glad to call him," she said.

Conrad frowned for a moment, then said, simply, "I'll let you know if I think that's necessary."

She nodded. "You know where to find me."

"I do."

A moment passed while they looked at each other, then finally Lily backed off. "Good night, Your Highness," she said, and started down the hall to the stairwell in order to avoid standing at the elevator banks waiting while he watched her.

"Good morning, Ms. Tilden."

Chapter Six

Conrad picked up the telephone several times and hung the receiver up again trying to convince himself to call Lily Tilden.

It might be a crazy idea, but on the other hand, it just might work. And if anyone was strong enough, and clever enough, and beautiful enough for the task, it was Lily.

In fact, she was all of those things in spades.

If he could convince her to go along with his plan, it might really help the Prince Frederick Foundation tremendously, to say nothing of what it could do to help his private life.

Finally he decided to just give it a try, and he lifted the telephone receiver and dialed zero to contact Lily.

She was the one who answered the call, and when he heard her voice he knew in his heart he was doing the right thing.

"Do you have a few moments?" he asked her.

He heard her shuffling papers on the other end as she said, "I have to take some magazines to Princess Drucille, and then I'll go directly to your suite."

His hand tightened on the receiver at the mention of Drucille, but he didn't say anything. "Thank you very much." He hung up the phone and paced the floor, wondering if he should reconsider his request to Lily Tilden.

When she got to the door, he still hadn't come up with a better plan and, in fact, had decided that if she wanted to refuse him and throw a glass of water in his face, well, it was a chance he was willing to take. It wasn't as if he was going to be here that long.

"I'm sorry it took me so long to get here," Lily said, looking at her watch. It had been twenty-five minutes since he'd called for her. "Your stepprincess Drucille had some additional requests when I got to her suite."

He could only imagine. "It's not a problem," he said, knowing full well he was in no position to be impatient with her timing. "I actually called you here to ask you for a favor."

"Okay…?"

"Actually, I have a proposal for you."

"A proposal." Lily shifted her weight from one foot to the other and folded her arms in front of her, a clear sign that she was preparing herself for the worst. "What is it?" she asked.

"Please—" he indicated the sofa "—take a seat for a moment and consider what I'm going to say carefully before you answer."

It seemed like forever that she eyed him and moved slowly to the sofa, but she did sit down, however gingerly. "You're making me a little nervous, Your Highness."

He smiled. "I can see that. And I thought you were the sort who never got nervous."

"Normally, I don't," she said, with a brief smile. "So maybe you ought to just tell me what it is you have in mind."

He decided to go straight ahead with his request first, and save the explanations for later. "I need a woman to pretend to be a companion to me this week. Someone the press could speculate about being a, how do you say it, a *love interest*."

Lily raised her eyebrows. "Are you asking me to find you a…hired escort?"

He wasn't from this country, but even Conrad knew that code. "No, no." He laughed. "That's not—no."

Her shoulders sagged with relief.

"What I'm asking…" He stopped, realizing that what he was asking sounded only a little less absurd and sleazy than asking her to procure a prostitute for him. "Let me back up a little bit. I'm here in New York to host a charity ball for my father, did you know that?"

She nodded.

"And there is the matter of an award for him at the United Nations as well."

"Yes," Lily said. "Friday afternoon, if I'm not mistaken."

"You're not." Conrad clapped his hands together once and tried to formulate the words quickly and easily. Unfortunately it was neither quick nor easy. He sighed. "I didn't always make my father very proud of me."

Lily looked surprised at this revelation. "You're probably being too hard on yourself," she said uncertainly.

He shrugged. "Perhaps. But I don't believe it was ever his desire for the royal family of Beloria to appear in the daily newspapers for their social exploits, but, unfortunately, it happened quite frequently with me."

"Youthful indiscretions?"

He smiled, embarrassed. "That's putting it kindly."

An uncomfortable moment of silence passed between them.

"We all have things in our past that we wish would just go away," Lily commented at last. "Fortunately, we don't all have those things covered by the local newspapers. But, really, how bad could you have been?"

He paused. "Suffice it to say, I've never been known as the humanitarian my father was. Anyway, all of this experience has given me a very clear understanding of how the media works with people like me. Truth doesn't matter much and charity doesn't matter at all. They want the promise of a fairy-tale romance at best or a sex scandal at worst."

Lily nodded. "I can see that."

"If I don't do something quickly, I'm afraid Brittany Oliver is going to take this opportunity to try and turn the press attention to some sort of scandal."

Lily looked disconcerted. "Does she have some sort of…ammunition?"

"What? Oh, you mean does she have a tape or pictures or something incriminating?" He managed to laugh at that. "Not at all. The time we spent together was strictly platonic. She approached me with a story about wanting to participate in the foundation." He shook his head. "As it turned out, it was not true."

Understanding lit Lily's eyes. "Which is why you wanted to avoid her."

"Exactly. But that didn't work out the way I'd hoped. My staff is still bringing me newspaper clippings and Internet gossip-site mentions."

"I'd imagine that happens a lot with you."

"Indeed, and it seldom matters. But this week it does. The foundation events this week were very important to my father, and he fully expected to be here. Now I need to proceed as he would have wished, as he would have *done*. And that does *not* include implications about myself and a fading Hollywood starlet."

Something in Lily's expression softened. "How can I help?"

"It's as I said at the beginning of our conversation. If I could be photographed with a young woman with more anonymity, it will serve to put out some of Brittany Oliver's fires. At the very least, it would cast considerable doubt on her stories of involvement with me."

"I see."

"It's a small thing," he acknowledged, "but effective."

"It makes sense," Lily said. "It's the same way with the hotel, actually. A small mention in the press can be better publicity than a costly advertisement. Only in our case it doesn't matter much whether it's a scandal or a nice mention."

He raised an eyebrow. It hadn't occurred to him that he might be able offer this as a mutually beneficial proposal. "Your understanding is most appreciated."

"So how can I help?"

He was glad she asked. "What I need, Ms. Tilden, is to have a woman—the *right* woman—to accompany me to the foundation ball on Saturday night, and to perhaps go to dinner or be seen out before that. Nothing overt," he hastened to add, "just someone to stand by and allow the press to conclude there is a romance where there is none."

"Well, there is no shortage of women who are willing to do that," Lily said. "In this hotel alone I could probably find at least three or four candidates, maybe more."

He knew who she was referring to. Lady Penelope. Baroness Von Elsborn. Probably a whole host of women just like them. "You don't understand," he said. "I need someone who is willing to see this as temporary, someone who won't imagine that there's something between us when this week is over."

"So you need an actress."

He imagined they both thought of Brittany Oliver at the same time, and he tipped his hand from side to side. "Maybe not an actress, per se, just someone a little less...hungry for romance."

Lily smiled. "I think I see your point. But I don't know how I can help you. I've done a lot of things under the wide umbrella of my job description, but finding fake girlfriends has never been one of my duties. I wouldn't even know where to begin."

"There is only one person I have in mind," Conrad said. "You can begin and end with her."

"Who?"

"You."

"*Me?*"

He nodded. "You'd be perfect for the job."

"But—but—but," she stammered helplessly, "but I *have* a job already!"

"I'll pay you four times your weekly salary just to go along with this for a week."

"If I go along with this plan I could lose my job entirely," she countered, still incredulous. "I'm sorry, but, no." She shook her head vehemently. "There's no way I could agree to that."

"You just said yourself that mention of this hotel in the press is better than costly advertising."

"That's true…but…"

"And it hasn't escaped my notice that the hotel does appear to be struggling somewhat as far as occupancy goes."

Her face flushed. "It's been a little rough lately."

"So just consider my proposition. Discuss it with the proprietor. I have a feeling you'll see this is mutually beneficial."

She sighed. "But why me? Of all the people out there who are much better at acting, and who are much more used to attending this kind of event, and frankly who are much more prominent socially, why do you want to use *me?*"

"Because you're the one I can trust not to give the truth away." He sighed and tried, again, to explain. "I don't want a girlfriend. I don't want romance. I don't want any sort of entanglements whatsoever." He looked at her imploringly. "It isn't that I'm asking for myself. If I were out to please myself, I could have done so easily."

She blanched at his indelicacy. "No doubt."

"Unfortunately, that is my talent," he said, flashing a quick smile, "but I'm asking you to help me bring attention—but not *too much* attention, or negative attention—to a very worthy cause." He shrugged and smiled again, with a shake of the head.

"I only know one way to create attention around myself, unfortunately. But I do believe in this case I might finally make that right."

She took a long breath in and held it for a moment before exhaling in one long hiss, like air going out of a tire. "I'm sorry. I understand what you're saying, but I just can't do what you're asking."

He nodded, more disappointed at the loss of her cooperation than he could admit. "I'm sorry to hear it."

"It's not that I don't want to help," she added. "I'm sure your father's charity is a wonderful cause and if there's any way I can help you with that while you're here I'm more than willing to do what I can. It's just…well…I don't think I can do…" She shrugged, clearly embarrassed. "You know, what you asked."

He almost laughed. "You do realize I was only asking you to stand beside me for the cameras. I mean, it wasn't as if I asked you to compromise your values."

Lily nodded. "That's true."

"What I've proposed is strictly business. And it's to benefit a charity, not myself or my personal holdings."

Lily's cheeks went pink. "I realize that—"

"Good. Regardless of your decision, I don't want there to be any misunderstanding."

She shook her head and stood to leave. "Not at all. And, honestly, I wish I could help you out, but

I'm just not very good at that sort of thing. I'm a lot better behind the scenes."

He waved her off. "Don't worry about it. There are other opportunities to bring the spotlight to my father's cause. I only asked this time because I am accepting the United Nations award for him this year and it would have meant so much for the Prince Frederick Foundation to get that extra boost of notice."

He thought she would leave, but she hesitated.

"What, exactly, is the Prince Frederick Foundation's cause?" She looked embarrassed. "I'm sorry, I haven't heard of it."

He smiled. "Exactly the problem. The foundation is, among other things, dedicated to funding research for juvenile arthritis."

"Oh." Her face grew serious. "Did your father suffer from arthritis?"

Conrad shook his head. "His younger brother did. It was a terribly sad thing. So little was known about what was wrong with him and he suffered far more than he needed to. My father never forgot that and when he was able, he decided to do something in his brother's honor."

"It's really nice that he had a way to honor his brother like that."

Conrad took a short breath. The loss of his father was still unexpectedly close. Sometimes it came over him in a rush and the emotion was thick. "He was like that," he said quietly. "He always wanted to help people. Some called him a weak ruler because of it."

"Some people just like to criticize those who are out there doing more for the world," Lily said gently. "You see that over and over again. Far more than you see someone who goes out there and makes an actual difference. It's really great that *you're* doing it now." She cocked her head and looked at him for a moment, started to say something, then shook her head. "You're not bad for a prince. In fact, whether you would or not, I'd call you a humanitarian."

He laughed. "May I quote you on that? The newspapers haven't mentioned that lately."

"Well, when you're a great-looking bachelor prince, the newspapers are really only interested in who you're seeing, not seeing, or who you're cheating on."

"You think I'm handsome?"

Her face flushed. "I didn't mean to—what I meant was…well, yes. I'm sure it's not the first time you've heard that."

"It's the first time it's interested me."

She looked into his eyes for a moment, giving him the chance to appreciate the brilliant blue of hers, then she said, "I have to go. I really have to get back to work."

"Thank you for your time."

She stood to go, smoothing her plain gray skirt down over slender thighs and hips. "Please don't hesitate to ask if there's anything else you need."

He gave her a long look. "You may be sorry you said that."

She laughed uneasily. "I often am."

He stood to escort her to the door. When he got there he opened it, and held it open while he looked down into those beautiful blue eyes again. Had he not been keeping the door open, he might have been tempted to kiss her. "Good night, Ms. Tilden. I've enjoyed our time together. I do hope you'll reconsider my offer."

"I'll think about it," she said, then looked into his eyes. "I honestly will. But I can't make any promises. Like I said, I think there are far better people for that kind of thing than me."

"You would be perfect."

He could have sworn her cheeks turned pink before she turned away and began walking toward the hall.

She stopped at the door and turned back to him. "Remember to call if there's anything else I can do." Then she hastened to add, "Theater tickets, events, arranging a private reception for you in your room, that sort of thing."

"Thank you."

"Okay, then." She seemed reluctant as she left, but she did go, closing the door quietly behind her.

Conrad watched her go and then watched the door for a few moments, musing over her attitude, before he went over and put the security lock in place.

The more he talked with Lily, the more he was

convinced she would be an asset to him at the charity ball on Saturday night. He hadn't planned on taking a date at all, but given the calls he'd already gotten from Brittany Oliver, the sudden appearance of Lady Penelope, and the strange little woman he kept running into in the halls who introduced herself as "Kiki," it occurred to him that he would be far better off with a date to dissuade their attentions.

Besides that, Lily had refused him. That, in and of itself, was a fair reason to win her over. It wasn't often that a woman refused him anything, just as Lily had said.

He found it intriguing.

The telephone rang and he looked at it with suspicion for a moment before crossing the room to pick it up.

"Yes?"

"Your Highness, it's Stephan. We have a bit of an issue threatening down here."

Brittany. It had to be. "What is it?"

"A woman who says her name is Kiki Von Elsen—"

"*Elsbon!*" the woman shrieked in the background.

"Kiki Von Elsbon," Stephan corrected, with exaggerated patience. "She came to the door and tried to use a credit card to unlock it," he said, chuckling softly, "as they do in the movies. Evidently she heard these were the royal quarters and she thought they were yours. What would you like for us to do?"

Conrad paused, and heard the woman screeching,

"I *told* you, I thought this was *my* room and I'd locked myself out!"

"Who is she?" Conrad asked.

"We have no idea, apart from what she's told us."

"Did you contact the front desk to find out if she's a guest?"

"We thought you might prefer us to contact you first."

Conrad sighed. "Give me a moment." He put the call on hold, then picked up the second line, dialed the operator and asked for Lily's extension.

She answered right away. "Lily Tilden."

"Ms. Tilden, my guards have apprehended a woman trying to get into their quarters. She said her name is Kiki Von Something. Do you know if such a person is a guest here?"

"Yes, she is." Lily's voice was tight. "I apologize for this. She is a guest here, I assure you."

"Is there any reason to believe she was confused when trying to enter the room downstairs with a credit card?"

"With a *credit card?*" Lily repeated. "You mean literally or was she trying to buy entrée?"

He laughed. "Literally."

"Good lord." She groaned. "I'll take care of this. Unless…you weren't planning on pressing charges, were you?"

"Not unless you think it's advisable."

"No, no, please. Ms. Von Elsbon is harmless. She just…doesn't always have good judgment."

That was an understatement. "Will you go to my guards' room and take care of this?"

"I'm on it."

"You're on it?"

He could hear the smile in her voice. "I mean, I'll be right there. Don't worry."

He had to admire her efficiency. Perhaps he *could* hire her to come back to Beloria with him and serve as his own private secretary, or social secretary, or some other position he had yet to invent. Whatever it was, he was certain she'd be good at it.

"Thank you, Ms. Tilden," he said, still mulling the idea. "You've been most helpful."

Chapter Seven

Lily spent the entire night and much of the next day replaying in her head her conversation with Prince Conrad. She had been really touched by his honor for his father, and his commitment to his father's charitable cause.

She'd really misjudged him at first when she saw him with Brittany Oliver. It had been too easy to conclude he was just another guy with money, power and position who was out to bed the cutest girl he could, without regard to who she was or what she was really like. Not that Lily could really make a personal judgment of Brittany Oliver, but given the stunt she'd pulled with the photographers, she didn't seem like a really stellar character.

But Conrad actually told Lily he didn't want this buxom young blonde hanging around him because he had more respect for his father than to let the attention be unduly swayed from his charity.

That was really rather surprising, actually.

And moving.

Having grown up without knowing anything about her parents, Lily had always been acutely aware of what a treasure it was to know what your heritage was, where you came from. She often felt like half a roadmap, showing the destination but nothing of how she got there. Who were her parents? What did they look like? Were they happy? Had they been healthy? Did her father hate lima beans like she did, did her mother love chocolate? Had Rose gotten her flair for cooking from one of their parents or grandparents? Where was her other sister?

It was just so hard to know nothing of her heritage.

So here was this man who had apparently spent a good portion of his life in pursuit of fun, but when it came down to it, he had valued his heritage more.

Lily liked that.

Maybe she *should* reconsider his request to pose as his date a couple of times, maybe it really *would* help him focus the attention on juvenile arthritis, rather than Brittany Oliver's career, or—heaven forbid—Kiki Von Elsborn's man-hungry advances.

Her sister Rose had told her to do it.

"It'll be fun!" Rose had insisted. "Look, how

often do you get a chance to come so close to being a real princess? It would be really glamorous."

"That's what I have you for," Lily had teased. Rose's husband, Warren Harker, was one of the wealthiest men in New York. There were plenty of opportunities for Lily to attend glamorous parties with Rose and Warren if she wanted to.

"I can offer you a lot of opportunities, but I can't offer you a date with a prince," Rose had said, laughing.

It was true. A date with a real prince. It might be an interesting story to tell her grandchildren one day. Or at least Rose's grandchildren, since she was actually married and getting ready to start a family.

The next morning, Lily told Gerard about Prince Conrad's offer and asked if it would be inappropriate for her to help him out that way.

"Darling Lily," Gerard said, "I would love for you to help His Highness out in whatever way you can." His expression grew serious. "Now, you know I would never *ask* you to do this, as it's certainly outside of your job description, but I would most certainly approve your participation if it would help the prince. Karen or Andy could add more hours to cut the slack when you're not here."

"It could also potentially help the hotel," Lily pointed out.

"I would not ask you to do anything that would make you uncomfortable on my behalf."

She smiled at him. "I know, Gerard, you never

have. But if it can help you—well, all of us here—
it's something I need to consider very seriously."

So Lily considered it.

However, she was so busy throughout the morning and the early afternoon that she barely had time
to think about it. First, three new guests had checked
in and needed to plan local travel for day trips as far
south as Washington, D.C. Then the child of one of
their guests had left a treasured teddy bear on the
subway near Coney Island. Fortunately, that was
Lily's home neighborhood, and she had a friend who
worked for the transit authority there. Thanks to him
and a sympathetic subway rider, the teddy bear had
been retrieved and messengered back to the Montclair, where he was given a "special bath" by Zipz
Cleaners two blocks down, and returned to his
owner.

If that wasn't enough, Kiki Von Elsborn had spent
the entire morning having Lily paged for one bogus
reason or another, always somehow leading back to
the subject of Prince Conrad and where he might be
dining for lunch or dinner.

It was exhausting.

She was about to take a fifteen-minute lunch—
and mental health—break when a young boy in a
wheelchair was wheeled in by a small but sturdy
woman who looked enough like him to almost certainly be his mother.

"Hello," Lily said, walking toward them. "Welcome to The Montclair, may I help you?"

"We're here to see the king," the boy said excitedly.

Lily looked at him and smiled. He must have been about six or seven years old at the most, and his pale gold hair and crystal blue eyes made him look like an angel. "The king?" she repeated.

"He means the prince of Beloria," the young woman explained, her cheeks flushing a light pink. "He asked to meet Jeff. My son," she explained, pointing toward the boy. "Jeff Parker?"

Lily hadn't heard anything about this visitor, but thanks to her conversation with Conrad last night she was able to put two and two together and figure out that Jeff might be in the wheelchair because of juvenile arthritis. "Are you involved with the Prince Frederick Foundation?" Lily asked the mother gently.

"Yes. Or they're involved with us. Jeff's teacher recommended him for assistance and they've really come through. He's been involved in the research program and last week he actually participated in Olympic Day at his school." The woman fluttered her hands in front of her. "Where are my manners? I'm Deena Parker." She held out her hand. "Are you part of the foundation?"

"Lily Tilden." Lily shook her hand. "No, I'm the concierge here at the hotel, but I am somewhat familiar with the foundation and with the work Prince Conrad is trying to do here."

"He's wonderful," the woman said, without a hint of the kind of swoon women usually used for men who looked like Conrad. "He really cares. Originally Jeff was going to meet Prince Frederick him-self this week, but, as you know…"

Lily nodded. "It's very sad." The cell phone on her belt buzzed and she said, "Could you excuse me a moment?" She answered the call and it was Karen, calling on behalf of Prince Conrad, who was looking for his guests. "Tell him I'll bring them up person-ally," she said, then clipped the phone shut. "His Highness will see you now."

"Is he really a king?" Jeff asked eagerly.

"Almost," Lily said, and Deena smiled gratefully at the kindness this stranger was giving to her boy.

"Does he wear silver armor?"

Lily laughed. "Not that I'm aware of. When you meet him, he'll look just like an ordinary man." Yes, the sort of ordinary man they chipped marble statues of in ancient Greece. "But he might have armor in his palace. I bet he has a royal shield anyway."

"Cool! And a sword?"

"I don't know. You should ask him."

Deena Parker blanched. "Oh, I don't think we should bother him with that sort of thing."

"He's really very approachable," Lily said to her in a quiet voice. "I'm sure he won't mind answering those kinds of questions." It was presumptuous of her to say so, she realized, but she *was* certain he wouldn't mind. From what he'd told her, he'd taken on the foundation because he cared and wanted to help people. If he was having this child in for a private meeting, it was because he wanted to have a meeting with a child. And only an idiot would think a kid wasn't going to want to know what it was like to be a prince.

She helped Deena get the wheelchair onto the elevator, and then pushed the button for Conrad's floor. The doors opened in no time and Conrad himself was standing there.

"I was just going down to look for you," he said, smiling at the mother, then looking straight at the child. "You must be Jeff."

Jeff nodded.

Conrad extended his arm to shake hands. "It is an honor to meet you, Jeff. I've heard so much about you. You're a real hero." His expression was soft as he looked at the child. "I'm Conrad, by the way."

"Are you the prince?"

Conrad shrugged it off. "Yes, but you can just call me Conrad."

"Lily said you have a shield in your palace."

Conrad raised an eyebrow and looked at Lily with an expression of amusement and surprise. "Did she?"

"Well, I—"

"She's exactly right," Conrad said pointedly. "It's huge and it's on the wall right over the fireplace in the Great Room."

"Is there a sword, too?" Jeff asked. "Like the one King Arthur pulled out of the stone?"

"There *is* a sword," Conrad said, "and the story is almost as interesting as King Arthur's. They say a swordsmith forged it in the fire of the sun seven hundred years ago."

If Lily had worried about the accuracy of her improvisation, this put her mind at ease.

Jeff's jaw dropped. "In the *sun?*"

Conrad shrugged. "That's what they say." He looked at Lily, and, upon seeing her expression, insisted, "That's what they say. It's legend in Beloria." His gaze lingered on her for a moment, then he turned to Deena. "I'm sorry, you must be Deena Parker."

She looked a little starry-eyed as she nodded. "Yes, that's right."

"Conrad," he said, then went on. "I have to say, you are a hero, too. I've read some of what you've gone through with your son and it obviously has been a difficult road."

Deena nodded. "But thanks to Prince Frederick, Jeff is so much better now than he was even a year ago."

Conrad looked so genuinely pleased that Lily felt something like pride in him. She told herself it was because it was so great to see someone care so much about people they'd never met.

And it was pretty cool to see a guy who had that sort of money and power—what a lesser man would use chasing ski bunnies at expensive European resorts—actually turning his energies to altruism.

They began walking down the hall toward Conrad's room and when they got to the door and he opened it, Lily said, "I'll let you off here, then. Please call if there's anything you need."

"Aren't you coming with us, Lily?" Jeff asked.

She deflected offers all day, but never from heartrendingly cute little kids. She looked to Conrad for help.

"Yes, aren't you coming with us, Lily?" he asked. "There's enough ice cream for you, too."

"Ice cream!" Apparently that was more interesting to Jeff than all the kings, and all the princes, and all the shields and swords in Europe. *"Wow!"*

Deena laughed, then said under her breath to Lily, "Please join us if you can. I'm a little nervous."

That did it. "Okay, but if my boss calls I'm going to have to go." She winked at Deena, who looked relieved.

They went into the suite, and Lily almost couldn't believe the sight before her. There were balloons everywhere, and a man standing there in a striped suit behind an old-fashioned ice-cream cart. On top of the cart there was every kind of ice-cream topping one could think of: peanuts, sprinkles, chocolate, caramel, butterscotch, whipped cream and beyond.

"I heard you like ice cream," Conrad said to Jeff with a shrug.

"Uh-huh." Jeff's eyes were wide as he took in the wide array of sweets.

From there, the conversation between Conrad and Jeff flowed. Conrad was excellent with the child, asking him what his father did for a living, how he liked school, what his favorite subjects were, and, eventually, how his illness affected him.

At one point, Conrad offered to show Jeff the view of Central Park from the west room and they excused themselves, leaving Lily and Deena to talk.

"He's amazing," Deena said, watching Conrad wheel her child into the next room. "A real natural with kids. You don't see that very often."

"No," Lily agreed, also watching them go.

"I just wish my husband could have been here to meet him." Deena sighed. "He had to work. His boss didn't want to let him off and he was too embarrassed to say he wanted to come meet a prince." She gave a laugh. "Too manly, you know."

Lily laughed. "I understand. As I'm sure you can imagine, most of the prince-watchers that have been coming around have been women."

"Oh, I bet," Deena said. "I read in some gossip column this morning that he's involved with Brittany Oliver, or whatever her name is, from that TV show about the crime-solving talking car."

"That's just a rumor," Lily said, inwardly rolling her eyes at the faint memory of *Crime Corvette*. "I haven't seen any evidence of him dating anyone at all, to tell you the truth. He's really involved in the work for the foundation."

"Isn't that something? You'd think a guy like that would be more interested in his social life. They usually are. Good-looking guys, I mean," Deena hastened to add. "I have no idea what royalty usually does."

Me neither, Lily thought. A lot of her preconcep-

OFFICIAL OPINION POLL

ANSWER 3 QUESTIONS AND WE'LL SEND YOU
2 FREE BOOKS AND A FREE GIFT!

0074823 ‖‖‖‖‖‖‖ ‖‖‖‖‖ ‖‖‖‖‖ FREE GIFT CLAIM # 3953

YOUR OPINION COUNTS!

Please check TRUE or FALSE below to express your opinion about the following statements:

Q1 Do you believe in "true love"?

"TRUE LOVE HAPPENS ONLY ONCE IN A LIFETIME." ○ TRUE ○ FALSE

Q2 Do you think marriage has any value in today's world?

"YOU CAN BE TOTALLY COMMITTED TO SOMEONE WITHOUT BEING MARRIED." ○ TRUE ○ FALSE

Q3 What kind of books do you enjoy?

"A GREAT NOVEL MUST HAVE A HAPPY ENDING." ○ TRUE ○ FALSE

YES, I have scratched the area below.

Please send me the **2 FREE BOOKS** and **FREE GIFT** for which I qualify. I understand I am under no obligation to purchase any books, as explained on the back of this card.

310 SDL EFZJ

210 SDL EFX7

FIRST NAME

LAST NAME

ADDRESS

APT.#

CITY

STATE/PROV.

ZIP/POSTAL CODE

www.eHarlequin.com

(STF-R-06/06)

DETACH AND MAIL CARD TODAY!

The Silhouette Reader Service™—Here's How It Works:

Accepting your 2 free books and mystery gift places you under no obligation to buy anything. You may keep the books and gift and return the shipping statement marked "cancel." If you do not cancel, about a month later we'll send you 4 additional books and bill you just $3.57 each in the U.S., or $4.05 each in Canada, plus 25¢ shipping & handling per book and applicable taxes if any.* That's the complete price and – compared to cover prices of $4.25 each in the U.S., and $4.99 each in Canada – it's quite a bargain! You may cancel at any time, but if you choose to continue, every month we'll send you 4 more books which you may either purchase at the discount price or return to us and cancel your subscription.

*Terms and prices subject to change without notice. Sales tax applicable in N.Y. Canadian residents will be charged applicable provincial taxes and GST.

If offer card is missing write to: Silhouette Reader Service, 3010 Walden Ave., P.O. Box 1867, Buffalo NY 14240-1867

BUSINESS REPLY MAIL
FIRST-CLASS MAIL   PERMIT NO. 717-003   BUFFALO, NY

POSTAGE WILL BE PAID BY ADDRESSEE

SILHOUETTE READER SERVICE
3010 WALDEN AVE
PO BOX 1867
BUFFALO NY 14240-9952

NO POSTAGE
NECESSARY
IF MAILED
IN THE
UNITED STATES

tions were being smashed by Prince Conrad. At this point she figured it was better to just watch and see, instead of trying to guess what sort of person he was and what that meant.

When he and Jeff came back in, Conrad was pushing the chair but Jeff was walking unsteadily behind him.

"Look at you!" Deena said, clapping her hands together and glowing with a mother's pride. "I thought you'd be too tired to walk so soon after physical therapy this morning."

"Nope. Conrad said he wanted to see me walk so I showed him."

Conrad gave an uncomfortable smile. "I actually meant it in the broad sense…but I hope this is okay."

Deena nodded reassuringly. "His physical therapist said he should do whatever he feels up to doing. The more he works those muscles, the better."

Jeff showed them all a couple of other cute, child-like tricks and they all applauded him. Even the ice-cream man had to wipe a tear off his cheek when Jeff reluctantly got back into his wheelchair for his mother to take him home.

"Thank you so much for a wonderful afternoon," she said to Conrad. Then she turned her gaze to Lily and added, "You, too, Lily. I don't usually come to fancy places like this but you really put me at ease."

Lily swallowed a lump in her throat. "It was fun," she managed to say. "Here, let me walk you down."

Deena waved the notion away with her hand.

"We'll be fine. You stay, eat your ice cream." She suddenly looked chagrined. "Unless, there's a policy against letting people wander the halls unescorted...?"

Lily could see that Deena was worried they'd want to keep an eye on her, so she sought immediately to put the woman at ease. "Of course not. If you don't mind, I'd love to stay here and have a banana split before I go back to work."

"You *should*," Deena said, with a broad smile. "Really."

They said their goodbyes and Conrad walked the mother and son over to the elevator and saw them safely onto it before coming back to Lily in the parlor.

"That was nice of you."

"*Me?* I didn't do anything."

He chuckled. "I notice you're still not eating ice cream."

She sighed. "No, you got me. I just didn't want her to feel she was being watched, like we didn't trust her or something."

"I know." He nodded. "I don't know where she got that idea but I'm glad you disavowed her of it so quickly." He smiled at her, the sort of smile that probably made some women's hearts leap. "You're very good with people."

She felt her face grow warm and glanced back at the ice-cream man, but he was busily putting everything away and wasn't paying any attention to them. "Thanks," she said to Conrad. "You, too. I was really impressed at how great you were with Jeff."

Conrad shook his head. "That's a special kid."

Lily stood up to leave. "He sure is."

"There are hundreds more in his position," Conrad said lightly, walking casually to the wet bar. "As you know, that's why I'm here. Donations made to the foundation have allowed Jeff to have two surgeries and all of his medications."

Lily knew what he was getting at. "It's a wonderful cause," she said tentatively.

Conrad cocked his head slightly. "Do I hear a note of concession in your voice?"

"I don't know what you mean."

He poured a glass of water and took it to her. "Yes, you do. Have you reconsidered my request that you play Cinderella to my Prince Not-All-Bad?"

She had to laugh. "I've thought about it."

He raised his brows and an unmistakable light came into his eyes. "And?"

She let out a long breath. "You're just talking about a couple of occasions, right?"

"Right."

"A couple of photo opportunities, and the charity ball on Saturday?"

"Exactly."

"No stories planted in the papers or scandalous scenes."

"Lord, I hope not." He held up his hand. "On my honor, that is not my intention or my wish."

She raised her chin and looked at him for a moment, considering, then said the words she'd been pretty sure she'd say ever since last night. "Okay, then, Conrad. You've got yourself a temporary fake girlfriend. Until midnight on Saturday."

"Only midnight?"

She shrugged. No point in belaboring the Cinderella references. "Or until the ball is over. Whichever comes first."

"Ah." He nodded. "I get it. Midnight. When I turn into a pumpkin. Or a mouse. Or something. I could never keep the story straight." He scratched his head in mock confusion. "Does the princess or fake girlfriend in this case fall asleep for a hundred years in the end?"

"Only if she's lucky," Lily said with a sigh. "Because this fake girlfriend could certainly use the rest. A hundred years seems just about right."

"I tell you what I'll do," Conrad said earnestly. "I'll arrange for a—" he thought for a moment "—a Caribbean cruise or something for you. A trip to Hawaii? Whatever appeals to you. To thank you for helping me out with this."

"That's not necessary."

"Please. I'd really like to do that for you."

Lily shook her head. "No way. You take the money you'd spend on that and put it right back into the foundation. That's payment enough for me."

He looked at her with something like admiration glowing in his eyes. "You're an unusual woman, Lily Tilden. A very unusual woman."

Chapter Eight

"I *knew* you'd do it," Rose said to Lily later that night as they sat on the floor of Lily's Brooklyn apartment, eating Rose's artichoke dip with homemade Parmesan crackers and drinking white wine.

"How did you know I'd do it? I didn't even know I was going to do it until I met that boy today."

"Yes, you did," Rose said, dipping a cracker and biting into it. "You *like* him."

"Oh, Rose!"

Rose laughed and began singing a song from *Cinderella*.

"Zip it, sis."

Rose stopped. "Come on, Lil, every girl loves a fairy tale. Especially this one."

"I'm *only* doing this to help out," Lily insisted. "It's *not* personal, honestly. Look at the newspapers—you can already see that they're focusing all sorts of negative publicity on his supposed exploits. Brittany Oliver has suggested there's a raunchy sex tape out there and I wouldn't be surprised if she went so far as to digitally alter one she already has." Lily shook her head and dipped a cracker. "It's pathetic. I really can see how much better it would be for him to have the appearance of a nobody at his side."

Rose reached over and mussed her sister's hair. "Aw, come on, Lil. You're not a nobody."

"You know what I mean."

Rose sobered. "Yes, I do. And I can see the merits of this plan, honestly. It's a good idea and I'm glad you're helping him out. But I still think you've got just a little bit of personal interest in doing it."

Lily looked at her. "Can we change the subject now, please?"

"Okay. I actually do have something important to talk to you about." She reached for her bag and pulled it over to her. "George Smith, Warren's private investigator, has come up with a little more information on our sister."

Lily's heart leapt. "Has he found her?"

"Not exactly." Rose took some papers out of the bag. "But he's found some information." She pulled a sheet of paper out and examined it. "Here it is. As of last June, she was working for an international aid foundation in eastern Europe." She passed it to Lily.

"What, like the Peace Corps?"

"Exactly."

Lily frowned and looked at the paper. "Laurel Standish." Tears burned in her eyes and she looked at her sister. "First a name, and now…now a job. A life. She's really starting to seem real."

Rose's eyes grew bright as well. "I know what you mean. When Warren first told me about her, it was an amazing concept but I don't think I really started to believe it fully until now."

Lily looked back at the papers. "She's obviously a really good person. Look at all this work she's done. She's a nurse." She gave a half laugh. "She's done us one better in the taking care of people department."

"At least we know it's a family trait."

"Grew up in upstate New York. Her mother died last year. Oh, that's sad. But her father's still up there." Excitement surged in Lily's breast. "Do you think we should go talk to him?"

"Absolutely. Oh! If she's still overseas, maybe we can at least see some pictures of her!"

"And get an address."

Rose nodded. "You know, for the first time, I really feel like we're *finally* going to get some answers. She may not know anything about our parents, but she's still the missing piece of our own puzzle."

Lily felt warm inside. "I can't wait. When do we go?"

"*After* your charity ball, Princess. Don't forget you still have work to do."

"I haven't forgotten."

"Good. Because I can't wait to hear how it goes. When does the big act begin?"

"Tomorrow, I guess." Apprehension lodged in Lily's breast. "Are you sure this isn't crazy?"

"Of course not! Seriously, you're just going to have a date or two with this guy in the public eye." Rose gave her most reassuring smile. "What's the big deal?"

The big deal arrived the next morning in the form of a white stretch limo. The driver came to Lily's door while she was still in a robe, her hair in a towel, and drinking coffee over the morning paper.

"Are youse Miss Tilden?" the driver asked, his New Jersey accent betraying him despite the austere uniform he wore.

"Yes?"

"A Prince Conrad sent me to pick you up for work."

She frowned. "Do you have some sort of identification?" She was used to dotting every *i* and crossing every *t*, whether it was at work or at home.

"Sure do." He took his license out of his pocket and handed it to her. "I also have a note for you." He took an envelope out of his other pocket. "I'll be downstairs when you're ready."

"Thank you," Lily said, then closed the door and went back to her kitchen to read the note over what was left of her cold cup of coffee.

Dear Lily,

I don't know you well, but I believe I know you well enough to know that your first inclination will be to refuse this ride into work. Please don't. You are doing me a tremendous favor, and I know it is at some expense to your own work schedule, so please allow me to make this one small gesture to make your life a little easier.

The driver will wait downstairs until you arrive or until I give him the message to leave without you. I hope it is the former and not the latter.

Yours, Conrad

Lily read the note over a couple of times and smiled. Yes, her inclination *was* to refuse the ride and go in to work as usual, but, yes, the ride *would* make her life a little easier. She wouldn't have to hurry as much to get into work.

She had to admit, she appreciated the fact that this man knew enough about her to acknowledge both of those things. As far as pretend boyfriends went, he was a pretty good one.

She got dressed quickly, even though she knew the limo driver would wait as long as his employer told him to, and she went down to the car. The neighborhood children had surrounded the car like ants, and the driver was playing it up, telling stories about how fast he could go in the limo and how cool it was to drive.

As soon as he saw Lily, he straightened up and cleared his throat. "My apologies, ma'am."

"Oh, no, go on!" Lily laughed. "It's not that often they get a show like this on this street."

He finished his story, in what was clearly a somewhat abbreviated manner, and told the kids he had to move the car so they had to get out of the way. The children scampered away, but kept their eyes on the oddity of a twenty-five-foot-long car as it drew silently away from the curb and moved down the street.

In the past, when Lily had been extravagant enough to hire a cab, she'd always felt every bump along the old road, but in the limo the ride was as smooth as a gondola sliding down the canals in Venice.

Before she knew it, the limo pulled up outside of the Montclair and, as she went to open the door, she was surprised to see not only the limo driver, but also Prince Conrad show up to open the door for her.

"I'll take care of this," Conrad said to the driver in a somewhat clipped voice. "You can go." He reached his hand in and helped Lily out of the car.

She was surprised at the multitude of camera flashes and clicks that went off. Somehow, when they'd pulled up she'd only had her eyes on Conrad and hadn't noticed the photographers and reporters around, but as soon as they went to work, she understood what her role was.

Conrad bent down to kiss her cheek, and she accommodated him, trying to ignore the clicks of the cameras and the calls of the reporters.

"Over here!"

"What's your name?"

"Is this your new girlfriend, Conrad?"

"Who is she?"

Conrad put his arm around Lily in a distinctly proprietary way and said, "This is Lily Tilden. She will be accompanying me to the Prince Frederick Ball in the Starlight Room on Saturday night."

"Are things serious between the two of you?"

Conrad's arm tightened around Lily's waist. "We're just friends," he said, in the way that countless movie stars had said before on the TV and Lily had never believed them, either.

"What about you, Miss Tilden. Did you work at this hotel before you got involved with His Highness?"

"That's how we met," she said smoothly, surprising herself with the ease of her response.

"Make sure you send your readers to *PrinceFrederickFoundation.com*," Conrad said, tightening his grip on Lily and guiding her gently toward the building.

"It's a really worthy cause," Lily added, then looked at Conrad.

He gave her a grateful smile and together they walked into the hotel without looking back, although Lily could definitely feel their lenses and their eyes trained on her back.

They went straight to Conrad's suite and it wasn't until they were there that Lily finally relaxed.

She plunked down on the sofa. "Okay, so that

was five minutes of what you go through all the time. How do you stand it?"

"I've had thirty-eight years to learn to ignore it if it began to bother me," he answered. "I think that helps."

"Well, there was definitely a comforting air of calm about you," Lily admitted. "If I hadn't been able to lean on you, literally, I don't know what I would have done."

"Don't worry," he reassured her. "You'll never need to know."

"Phew!" She leaned her head back. "Honestly, I'd have to be really in love with a guy to put up with that." She heard her own words and realized how rude they might sound. "Not that it would be that hard for a woman to put up with that in order to be with you."

He laughed. "A woman would have to be crazy to put up with that if she didn't have to. No matter what the reason."

"Oh, there are plenty of women who would find it worthwhile." Lily shrugged. "It wasn't *so* bad."

"You hated it."

A moment pulsed between them.

"Yeah," she admitted at last. "I sort of did. But then I've never liked being the center of attention. Simple as that. Truthfully, that probably makes *me* the weirdo. You only need to watch ten minutes of the morning news shows to see there are crazy idiots everywhere who would do just about anything to get three seconds in the camera's focus."

"I believe I've met some of them," he said cryptically.

Lily didn't push for an explanation. It was likely he was referring to Princess Drucille or Lady Ann. Or possibly Lady Penelope, who had spent a great deal of time these past couple of days hanging around the lobby and elevator banks looking blank and lost, yet springing to animated life every time the elevator doors opened, only to have her expression crumple every time it wasn't Conrad.

"So how do you find someone to marry under these circumstances?" Lily asked him, leaning back against the sofa.

He looked surprised at her question. "I don't know. As you can see, I've never married."

"Does that mean you're never going to marry?" she persisted. She didn't know what made her so bold, but she was definitely curious about the answers so she did not rescind the questions.

"No," he said quickly, then reconsidered for a moment and added, "I hope not. It just takes the right woman."

"And what would she be like?"

Conrad turned skeptical eyes on Lily. "You're very curious all of a sudden."

She smiled. "If five minutes in the spotlight has done that to me, just think how bad it will be Saturday when I spend the whole evening as your date."

Conrad looked at her seriously for a moment,

then the trace of a dimple dented his cheek. "You're goading me, aren't you?" he asked, pointing at her.

"A little, maybe," she admitted reluctantly.

"You're a very difficult woman sometimes, you know, Miss Tilden."

"I've heard that," she confessed. "Sometimes."

He watched her for a long moment, then said, "It's interesting to me. In my country, all the women know who I am and have ideas about what it would mean to be Crown Princess of Beloria. I seldom get to meet a woman who has no interest whatsoever in taking on that role."

Lily felt her face grow warm. "Well, believe me, I have no interest in taking on that role."

His facial expression didn't change. "I believe you," he said. "That's why it's such a relief to be around you."

She laughed out loud at that assertion. "You do realize you're saying you like being around me because I'm not the kind of girl who wants to spend that much time around you."

The dimple showed up in his cheek again. "I guess I am," he admitted, then chuckled. He went over and sat down next to her. "At least I know you're in agreement."

"Absolutely."

"Good. So where shall we go for dinner tonight?"

Lily swallowed. She knew that she was going to spend a few days pretending to date Conrad, but it still made her feel a little funny to actually take off work and do it.

"You're not having second thoughts, are you?" he asked, as if reading her mind.

"No," she answered quickly, and realized that she meant it. No, she wasn't having second thoughts. Sure, she felt a little nervous about actually going out on the town with this famous and powerful man and, no, she didn't particularly like having her photograph taken.

But despite all of that, she really liked Conrad. He had a way of putting her at ease and she really appreciated it. As uncomfortable as it was to be around him in public, it was extraordinarily comfortable to be with him in private.

It was confusing.

"I'm not having second thoughts," she said, unable to fully express the dichotomy of her feelings. "It's actually very…interesting."

He raised an eyebrow. "Really?"

She nodded. "Really. I don't think I'll ever get this kind of star treatment again."

"It's funny you should say that," Conrad said, looking into her eyes, "because I've been thinking these past few days that I might never be lucky enough to meet someone who just treats me normally again. The way that you do."

"Who gives you a hard time, you mean," she teased.

His expression remained serious. "In a way, perhaps I do. Where I come from, people are afraid to give me a hard time. There is a lot of yes-ing, and agreement, and I often wonder what they say when they walk away." He smiled. "But I'll never know."

Lily softened toward him. "It never occurred to me that it might be difficult to have people so reverent toward you."

He made a face. "I don't mean to complain. Obviously there are a lot of benefits as well. I live a very comfortable life. In fact, until I came here, I didn't realize exactly what was missing."

Lily looked at her hands and tried to come up with an appropriate response, but nothing came to her beyond, "I'm sorry to hear that."

Conrad leaned toward her. She felt the heat from him before she felt the touch of his hand on her cheek.

She turned to face him, and he cupped her cheek with his hand. "You are so beautiful," he said to her, his green eyes penetrating, studying her, almost as if he was memorizing her features. "I wish I had more time to stay and get to know you."

"There's not much to know," she said, a little breathless.

He shook his head. "That is not so." Then he lowered his mouth onto hers.

The kiss filled her senses with a delirious feeling of exhilaration. The moment his lips touched hers, she felt her heart *whoosh* just like it did when she rode the Cyclone at Coney Island as a kid. And just as it was on the roller coaster, Lily's feelings were a mingling of fear and pure joy, both teetering on two ends of a scale. The balance of emotion tipped one way and then the other with such speed that she could only feel and not give in to thought.

And she did. She drank in the taste of him, inhaled the masculine sense of him, and when he put his powerful arms around her and drew her close, she surrendered completely to the safety and security of his strong embrace.

Suddenly he wasn't a prince, and she wasn't a pauper; she was a woman and he was a man…an intensely charismatic, magnetically attractive, powerfully masculine man.

"We shouldn't do this," Lily tried to object, in between breathless kisses. "We have a business arrangement."

Conrad drew back for a moment. "You don't imagine I think this is part of the deal, do you?"

She took a breath, wishing the flush would leave her cheeks. "Oh, no, I didn't mean that—"

"Good." He kissed her again, more hungrily than before.

She sank against him, allowing herself another few moments of this exquisite pleasure before insisting that they return to a more detached, professional relationship.

But it wasn't so easy. Conrad's kisses were like none she'd ever experienced before. For a girl who had spent her whole life feeling like a misfit, unsure of where she'd come from or where she belonged, something about Conrad fit.

Which was crazy, because he was a prince, for crying out loud! His family had spent the past seven or eight centuries ruling a European country. He was part of *history*. Where her place in the world was a tiny little question mark, his place was a great big exclamation point, right there in the history books.

If she allowed herself to feel something for him, she was just setting herself up for a fall. There was no way he was ever going to take her seriously. They didn't have a future. They didn't even have a present. All they had was a few more days of charity work together. It didn't amount to anything other than that.

And she was a fool if she imagined otherwise.

She pulled back more firmly this time, reseating herself a few inches back. "We can't," she said, even though she knew her eyes and her lips were telling him *we can*.

Fortunately he was a gentleman and he listened to what she said. "Is something wrong?"

She shook her head, feeling the blood rise in her cheeks for the second time in the past ten minutes. "I'm just not the kind of girl who can just…do that—" she gestured helplessly at the space between them "—for fun. I can't just have a fling."

"Lily." He took her hands in his and forced her to look at him. "I would never use you that way."

"I didn't mean to suggest you wanted to *use* me," she objected, feeling like everything she said just made things worse. "But you're leaving in a few days, and even if you weren't…" She shrugged. "You'd still be leaving. And I just don't want to feel…sad about that."

A smile tugged at the corner of his mouth. "You honor me with your words."

She sighed. "I sound like a fool."

He reached over and touched her cheek again, running his thumb along her jawline. "No, you don't. But I will respect your request. I understand. And you're right, of course, I'll be leaving to go home, three thousand miles away, in just a few days. There is no point in starting something we cannot continue."

As if he'd be able to *continue* a relationship with an American who had nothing in the way of a pedigree anyway. "So we agree."

He didn't back away and she didn't want him to. "We agree."

She swallowed, trying to will herself to stand up or back up or, for heaven's sake, even fall right off the sofa—anything to widen the gap between them before she threw herself into his arms.

"Okay, then." She tried to catch her breath. "As we were saying earlier, where should we go for dinner? I expect you want someplace intimate yet visible enough to prove we're together."

He looked impressed. "Perfect. What do you have in mind?"

She could do this in her sleep. "Hitchcock's," she suggested. "On Amsterdam. It's a nice little place, just elegant enough to comfortably host someone like you—"

He sighed.

She smiled. "Yet not too interested in being exclusive. I think it will do nicely."

He nodded. "Eight o'clock?"

"You've got it. I'll go down to my office and make the arrangements."

"Always the professional."

She shrugged and stood up, reflexively smoothing her clothes. "It's what I do."

"I have one more request."

"What's that?"

"I'd like to have a personal shopper come from Melborn's department store to talk to you about what you'd like to wear to the ball."

"That's not necessary." But…wasn't it? She didn't have anything really suitable to wear to an event like this. Even Rose didn't usually go to things as fancy as this ball promised to be.

Lily could have demurred, but the fact was it was Prince Conrad's reputation on the line, not hers. She had to look right for the part. He was aware of that. She needed to respect that and go along with it. She wasn't all that comfortable letting a man buy her clothes, but under the circumstances, it would have been selfish of her to refuse.

"But if it would make you feel more comfortable, that's fine," she amended.

"I'm certainly more comfortable making this easier for you, if possible. I wouldn't want you to have to trouble yourself anymore than necessary. This way you can come back up to my suite this afternoon and relax while the shopper learns your tastes and brings you some garments to choose from." He smiled. "Is that all right with you?"

"Fine." She headed toward the door. "What time is convenient for you? I can arrange to have them come around two or so, if that works."

Conrad shook his head. "You're doing enough. Let me handle this. Two o'clock it is."

Lily wasn't used to letting other people take over the work, especially when it came to doing the very things she spent all day doing for hotel guests. But Rose was constantly telling her she had to give up control just a little, every once in a while, and this was a good example of what she meant.

"I'll see you then," she said with a light smile, then turned on her heel and headed down the hall, giddily conscious of his gaze upon her all the way to the end, where she got on the elevator.

Chapter Nine

"So that's dinner for three at Hitchcock's at eight o'clock?" Karen was saying into the telephone when Lily got to the office. "Princess Drucille, Lady Ann and Lady Penelope…yes, I've got it. Very good, Your Highness. No, I'm sure there won't be any problem." She hung up the receiver then picked it up again and was about to begin dialing when Lily spoke.

"You're kidding, right?" Lily asked, flabbergasted.

Karen looked puzzled. "About what?"

"About making reservations for Princess Drucille and company at Hitchcock's."

Karen frowned. "Lily, what are you talking about?"

Lily shook her head. "I'm sorry, it's just an amazing coincidence. I was *just* talking to Prince Conrad about going to Hitchcock's at eight for dinner and when I came down here you were making reservations. For them." It was almost uncanny. But surely Princess Drucille hadn't managed to put *another* microphone into his room. Now that he was aware that she'd done it, he wasn't letting her anywhere near his suite.

Still, there was something strange about it. "I think I'll have to suggest an alternate for Conrad."

"*Ooh,* Conrad, is it?" Karen giggled. "Getting quite close, aren't you?"

"That's what the world is supposed to think," Lily said, giving her friend a brief overview of the situation.

"I've got an idea," Karen said when Lily had finished. "Remember Chef Antonio from Maggie's?"

Lily nodded.

"He's just opened a fabulous new place downtown. Bell'arrivo. The food is fabulous, the atmosphere is gorgeous—very flattering light—and it's in the exact opposite direction of where the princess is going."

Lily snapped her fingers. "You're brilliant. I'm doing it."

"No," Karen said, putting a hand on Lily's forearm. "Let *me* make the reservations. This is your week to be treated like a princess."

Lily smiled. It was beginning to feel as if Christmas had come a month early. "Thanks, Karen. You're the best." She went back into the office and dialed Conrad's suite. He answered on the second ring. "Look, I was just talking to Karen and she suggested another restaurant. Do you mind if I change our arrangements?"

"Not at all," he said. "Whatever pleases you."

Those were potentially dangerous words. "Okay. Don't worry, you won't be sorry you said that."

"I'm sure I won't. By the way, I called Melborn's department store and they said they were sending someone named Maureen over at two. I'll be leaving in just a bit, so please use your key to get in."

"It's not necessary," Lily said. "I can use another room." But she couldn't, the hotel was completely booked. Still, they could squeeze into the office—

"I insist," Conrad said in a clipped voice. "Enjoy yourself and I'll see you later." He hung up before Lily could object further. She had the feeling maybe that was on purpose.

She sighed and sat back in the leather executive chair she'd talked Gerard into getting a few months ago. He'd joked that it was almost comfortable enough to sleep in, but Lily did find herself nodding off as she sat there. But she didn't think she'd actually fallen asleep until she woke with a start—and a sore neck—and looked at the clock on the desk. It was already quarter after two!

She ran from the office and to the elevators, pressing the button impatiently until the doors finally opened. She got to Conrad's floor just as a slight, effete young man was preparing to get on the elevator.

Lily started to pass him, then, possessed of an instinct, she stopped and turned back. "Excuse me," she said. "You're not, by any chance, here from Melborn's department store, are you?"

The young man looked at her and got off the elevator. "You're not *Lily,* are you?"

She nodded. "Yes, I am."

He sighed dramatically. "Well, I *do* have my work cut out for me. Just look at that hair!"

She glanced at herself in the mirror on the wall. He was right. Her hair was a mess. All bent and snarled where she'd leaned against the chair as she slept. "I'll get a brush," she said, but he stopped her.

"Honey, you're not getting a *brush,* you're getting a *makeover.*"

"What? I thought you were a personal shopper."

"Personal *stylist,* honey, and it looks like I got here just in the nick of time." He took Lily by the arm and began to pull her along toward Conrad's suite.

"Wait a minute," Lily said. "I thought they were sending *Maureen* over."

He stopped and put his hands on his hips. "My *name,*" he said, with exaggerated patience, "is *Maurice.*"

"Ah." She nodded. She could see how Conrad might have misunderstood that. "All right, but… nothing too radical."

He just glanced at her over his shoulder and snorted.

An hour later, Lily found herself at the trendy Daniel Salon downtown, her hair covered in foil and highlighting cream. A manicurist sat at her side doing her nails, while a flamboyant young man named Freddy finished painting on the highlights.

"I can't believe you've never done this before," Freddy said. "You're going to just love it. I know, I know, you probably thought your hair was too pale to need highlights, but here's what I've done—some pillowcase platinum highlights on the top and around your face, but I've added deeper caramel highlights to the sides and back. You're going to look just *gorgeous.*"

"And you need to," Maurice added, from where he was watching several feet away. "Page Seven said this morning that there's some sort of Lady Snooty staying at the hotel trying to win your man."

Page Seven. Caroline Horton's column. "Lady Penelope?"

Maurice snapped his fingers. "That's her! The picture was blurry but she looked a bit bovine to me."

If the picture was blurry, it was probably on purpose, Lily thought. "He's not *my man,*" she said, instead of delving into the subject of Lady Penelope. "This is just for one night."

"One magical night." Maurice looked pleased as punch. "That's how it begins. Which is why we need to make you as absolutely gorgeous as possible."

"Not hard," Freddy interjected.

Lily looked skeptically at Maurice. "I'm not sure this is what Prince Conrad had in mind when he sent you over."

"Honey, Mr. Prince didn't know what you'd want so he said to give you carte blanche. He said if you wanted a whole new wardrobe you were to have it, so here you are."

Lily had never accepted such generosity from a man before and it made her uncomfortable, even while it thrilled her.

She'd arranged days like this countless times for clients at the hotel, but she'd never dreamed of actually having one for herself. After wrestling with it for half the afternoon, she finally decided to give in.

By 5:00 p.m. she looked like a whole new woman. Her hair, which had previously hung long and straight, was cut into face-framing long layers and the color was alive with spun gold lights.

Maurice had also subjected her to the painful process of having her eyebrows waxed and plucked into a new shape that framed her blue eyes and made her look elegant and sophisticated.

The change, though subtle, was exciting.

Afterward, Maurice stated that he'd gotten a sufficient idea of her personality and sent her back to the suite to wait for him while he pulled a selection of dresses from the designer vault at Melborns.

She went back to the Montclair feeling self-conscious about the change in her appearance. It was a sensation that wasn't helped much by the reactions of her coworkers.

"Holy cow, you are a knockout!" Andy exclaimed. His eyes were wide with appreciation. "I knew you were pretty, Lily, but you look like a movie star."

Her face felt warm. "Stop it, Andy."

"I'm serious." He called to Gerard in the back office. "Gerard, come get a look at our girl."

"Why do I feel like I'm on display in the zoo all of a sudden?" Lily asked.

Andy *pshh'd* her and Gerard emerged from the back with a gasp. "My goodness, you truly are a vision."

"Thank you, Gerard." This was getting really embarrassing.

"Show Karen," Andy said.

"I've really got to go do a couple of things," Lily said. "I'll see her later."

Finally she was able to extract herself from the circle of inspection that the lobby had become. She went back to the suite and sat on the sofa to recharge her batteries. She'd been in here a hundred times when there was no guest, but today it felt different. It was as if it had ceased being a suite in the Montclair and had become, instead, an extension of Conrad. It felt like him, suddenly, instead of just feeling like her place of work. The difference was interesting and she was enjoying it when Maurice came back with his trendy young assistant, Cho.

There followed an hour of trying on dresses and

accessories. Lily felt as if she were in a movie, twirling in front of the mirror, staring at a woman who looked only vaguely familiar. She finally settled on a deep royal blue silk dress for the ball. It was a little different, as formal gowns went, and when she first saw the dress, she was skeptical.

"Just try it on," Maurice said confidently. "Don't judge it until you see it on."

She tried it on and he was right. It was a dream. The color was perfect on her, highlighting the blue of her eyes and complementing her skin tone in a way she wouldn't even have imagined possible. The cut was flattering, though a little long, but Maurice assured her that could be taken care of easily.

"This is the one, isn't it?" he said enthusiastically. "It's a Toresti original, only seen once on the runway in Milan. You'll knock them dead, Lily, you really will."

"It's beautiful, for sure," Lily said, admiring the beautiful garment. "I don't think anyone would look bad in it."

Maurice snorted at the very idea, then said, "And I have the perfect outfit for you to wear to dinner tonight. It's a sort of retro, Mary Tyler Moore on the *Dick Van Dyke Show* number, with—"

"Wait a minute," Lily said. "I can't spend any more of this man's money. I'm not sure we should have done everything we've done so far, but all I really needed was a dress for Saturday night and now I have that, so we just can't keep going."

Maurice looked at her impatiently and put his hands on his hips. "The instructions to me were to provide you with everything you could possibly want or need. And, honey child, believe me, you *need* this outfit. It will be *killer* on you." He must have seen the objection rising in Lily's throat again, because he held up his hand and said, "Okay, okay, just try it on. Let me see it on you since I brought it over. *Indulge* me."

Lily sighed and paused for a moment before nodding. "Fine. I'll try it on. But then you're taking it back with you and I'm going back to work to get a few things done before I leave tonight."

"Fine." Maurice snapped his fingers and Cho jumped to do his bidding. She dug through the clothes and pulled out an all-black outfit which, on closer inspection, was a pair of cigarette-style silk pants and a light, form-fitting black cashmere mock-turtleneck sweater. It was a deceptively simple ensemble, considering the fact that it had a Lyle Ridgeville label and probably carried a ticket price of several thousand dollars. "Go on." Maurice shooed her away. "Give it a whirl."

Lily smiled at his quirkiness and went into the powder room to change. When she had the outfit on, she almost couldn't believe the sight before her in the mirror. It fit like a dream, slimming wherever she was slim and embracing her curves in such a way as to make her feel voluptuous and beautiful, like Marilyn Monroe or Lana Turner.

She stepped out of the powder room. "You're right," she told Maurice, "it's really pretty ni—"

"Stop the presses!" Maurice shrieked. "Grace Kelly has a successor and her name is Lily Tilden."

"Oh, good grief, Maurice, give it a rest." Lily smiled. "It's not that big a deal."

"Not that big a deal!" He looked to Cho, who nodded in response.

His exclamations were cut off by the electronic sound of a keycard in the door. Everyone looked as Conrad walked in, looked up at them all and asked, "What's wrong?"

"Nothing," Maurice answered, in the voice of a guilty four-year-old child.

"We were just talking about whether or not I need this outfit," Lily answered. "And, of course, I don't."

Conrad looked her up and down, sending shivers of pleasure through her. "Why not?"

"Because…" How could she explain what seemed so obvious? "It's not necessary. The dress for the ball, okay, I can see that, but this…" She gestured over her figure. "This is just casual."

"And perfect for your dinner tonight," Maurice sniped.

Conrad shot him a look. "He's right. It is." Then he looked at Lily. "By the way, who is he?" He looked at Maurice. "Who are you?"

"Maurice Gibbons. You sent for me through Melborn's department store."

Conrad looked vaguely surprised. "Oh. I thought

that was…of course. Maurice. Exactly who they said we should expect."

Maurice looked satisfied with that, and, with his confidence renewed, said, "So don't you think she should keep the ensemble and wear it out to dinner tonight?"

Conrad looked befuddled. "Whatever she wants."

"Well, she'd better want this, if she knows what's flattering for her," Maurice said.

Lily stifled a laugh. Maurice was right, of course, the outfit was most definitely flattering. He knew his stuff. But even more than that, Lily could understand Conrad's confused state of mind. He didn't know anything about women's clothing, and he was clearly ready to agree to whatever made her happy.

That, in itself, made her happy.

Not because she wanted stuff, heaven knew, but because she hadn't known too many men who were more interested in her desires than in their own.

"I don't need the outfit," she said firmly, and turned to go back into the powder room to change.

"Wait." Conrad's voice was so commanding she had to stop.

"Yes?" She stood before him and looked into his eyes.

"Do you like it?"

She hesitated. "Maurice has excellent taste."

"But do you like it? Do you *want* it?"

"I like it," she said. "But I do *not* need it."

Conrad looked at Maurice. "Add it to the bill."

"Done," Maurice responded quickly.

An objection rose in Lily's throat. "Wait, you can't—"

"Should I send the receipt to you here?" Maurice asked Conrad, totally ignoring Lily.

"No! Seriously, don't—" Her objection was squelched by Conrad's response.

"Yes, send it here." Then, to Lily, he said, "Stop trying to stop this. I want you to have it. Wear it tonight, I like the look. If you never wear it again, fine, give it to charity. But, please, let me do this for you."

She heard his words but was unsure of the subtext. Was he telling her he'd rather make sure she was dressed appropriately tonight, even if he had to pay for everything, or was this just his way of trying to make her feel more comfortable about what was obviously a ticklish situation?

She had no idea.

All she knew for sure was that he was making her feel like a genuine princess. Maybe better, maybe a queen. In any event, he was making her feel valued, and that was worth more than anything she'd ever had.

So if he wanted her to wear this incredibly flattering outfit—or *ensemble,* as Maurice would say— then she would.

And she would enjoy every moment of it.

Chapter Ten

That night, Lily and Conrad went to the restaurant in style, in a black stretch limo, complete with cold champagne and Frank Sinatra music piped quietly in through surround sound speakers.

Lily leaned back against the leather seat and breathed in the heady scent of leather and Conrad's aftershave. "This is really fun, I have to admit," she said to Conrad. "When I was a little girl I used to see these big, sleek cars humming around town, but I never thought I'd be on this side of the tinted glass. You must love being able to ride everywhere in style like this."

He smiled a little sadly. "The truth is, I'd rather drive myself or walk whenever possible, but sometimes the occasion calls for transportation and it's easier to secure a limousine than a regular car."

"Secure?"

He nodded and poured a glass of champagne. "Bulletproof glass, hidden guards when necessary, that kind of thing."

Lily's jaw dropped. "Is that sort of thing necessary?"

"Almost never in my country, but here it's better to take the precautions sometimes." He handed her the glass. "Particularly in recent years."

Lily nodded, sad at the truth of it. "So tell me, what is Beloria like?"

"It's beautiful," he said. "Rolling hills dotted with small farms, villages with lots of shops and artisans, always a clock tower in the town square." He looked out the window. "It's exciting here, but I miss the quiet beauty."

"I can imagine." Lily took a sip of the fine champagne and set the glass down. "When I was young I loved books about places like that. I would dream of sitting on a green, green hill in the spring with nothing but wildflowers and blue sky and white clouds."

"Then you should come visit in the spring," Conrad said with a smile. "And I promise to make your dream come true. We have many such places."

The car slowed and drew to a halt outside Bell'arrivo. A clutch of photographers stood huddled out front.

"Are they here for you?" Lily asked.

Conrad took a slow, patient breath. "I'm afraid so. Your colleague Karen made the call to several papers, to let them know we'd be here. Don't worry, it will be over quickly."

Lily looked out the window at the photographers again and swallowed. This had seemed easy in theory, but now these people were going to take her picture emerging from the car. The opportunities for unflattering shots were numerous, and the possibility of former boyfriends seeing them and feeling smug was too real.

"Are you okay?" Conrad asked quietly.

"Yes, fine." Lily smiled, amused at her own vanity. This wasn't about her, it was about the Prince Frederick Foundation. She was only there to help put the spotlight on Conrad.

The driver opened the door, and Conrad got out first so he could assist her out and guide her through the paparazzi.

"Prince Conrad!"

Several flashes popped, their neon echoes floating in Lily's vision for a couple of moments afterward.

"Is this the new woman in your life?"

"Are things serious?"

"What happened to Brittany Oliver?"

"Does this mean the rumors about you and Lady Penelope aren't true?"

Conrad answered the questions in turn, masterfully spinning them so that he ended up talking about the foundation and the upcoming charity ball. He managed to do it without sounding preachy or like an advertisement for good deeds. Indeed, he managed to make it all sound so intriguing that if Lily were not already a part of it, she'd be wondering what would happen next.

When the last question was answered, and the last flash had gone off, Conrad thanked them for letting himself and Lily have some privacy and waved as he ushered her into the restaurant.

"They're not leaving you know," she said under her breath as they walked in. "They'll just press their cameras against the glass and hope to get a good picture."

"Mmm-hmm," he responded lowly. "And, with your permission, I'd like to give it to them."

Lily's heart thrummed in response, but she didn't know what to say. "We'll have to negotiate that," she joked.

"You don't make things easy, do you?"

"Of course I do, it's my job."

He laughed.

They were seated at a private table in an alcove at the end of the restaurant. There was a clear shot to the front window, but at least there were no tables close enough to theirs for the patrons to hear what they were saying.

As soon as the hostess had left them with their menus, Conrad said, "Thank you again for doing this. I know you didn't want to."

"Actually, it's not so bad."

He looked surprised. "No?"

"Not at all." She hesitated while a busboy filled their goblets with sparkling mineral water. "As a matter of fact, I'm kind of enjoying it."

"I'm glad to hear it. Surprised, but glad. I imagined you'd find all of this quite tiresome. You didn't look all that thrilled when I told you the stylist would be coming over."

Lily laughed. "Well, that's true. I could do without that part of it, but it was a good feeling to stand beside you out there, knowing that we were doing something really worthwhile. And meeting little Jeff the other day…" She sighed. "What you did meant so much to him and to his mother. It was very exciting to be a part of that, albeit a very small part."

"I was extremely grateful to have you there," he confessed. "The child was easy, but I think I would have been at a loss talking to the mother on my own. I'm not very good at small talk."

"That's not true, you did great."

The conversation flowed from there, as did the mineral water. They went through three full courses and dessert before Lily looked at her watch and saw, with a shock, what time it was. "My goodness, it's after midnight!"

"Do you have to be somewhere else?"

"No, it's just…I had no idea that so much time had passed." She glanced toward the window, where she could still see a few photographers waiting. "Those poor guys must be freezing!"

Conrad followed her gaze and nodded, then he summoned the waiter. "There are some photographers outside—"

"I'll get rid of them right away, Your Highness."

"No, no, I just want you to go offer them cappuccinos. On my check, of course."

The waiter looked astonished. "I'm sorry, did you say you want me to offer them coffee? On your bill?"

"Yes."

Lily watched with amusement as the befuddled waiter went outside, jotted orders, and came back into the kitchen.

"He's confused because he didn't expect you to be nice," Lily commented with a laugh. "Believe me, we've had some royalty and some dignitaries come stay at the hotel and they are usually…well, they tend to be a little egocentric."

"Like my father's wife."

Lily shrugged, knowing she couldn't badmouth a customer no matter how much she agreed with his assessment. "There have been a lot of them."

Conrad gave a nod, signaled the waiter for the check, then returned his attention to Lily. "You must have dreaded it when you heard I was coming."

She smiled. "Of course not. We all knew it would be interesting. I had no idea it would be quite *this* interesting, though."

"If hotel work doesn't hold your interest, you could always have a career in the theater," Conrad said. "You've been marvelous."

"I doubt there's an Oscar in my future."

The waiter appeared and discreetly laid the check on the table. Conrad took cash from his wallet, slipped it in the folder, and pushed it to the edge of the table.

"Are you ready?" Conrad asked.

"Sure." She stood up, and realized afterward that she was expected to wait for him to pull her chair back for her. It was as she'd said, she wasn't *that* good in her role.

They walked to the coat check at the front of the restaurant and Lily could see that the photographers, now caffeinated, had resumed their positions, ready to take pictures.

Conrad must have noticed it, too, because he helped her with her coat, then kept his arms on her shoulders. "I think this would be a good moment for a kiss," he said quietly.

"It would probably catch their interest," she agreed.

"Do you mind?"

No, she didn't mind. Not this time, since it was just pretend. It wasn't as if she was going to feel anything. It wasn't real.

She kept telling herself that, as he pulled her into his arms and kissed her. And, just like that, the world around them seemed to disappear. The noise of the restaurant, the tinkling of glasses and plates, the muted conversations—all of it, gone.

There was nothing but this man's warm embrace, and the feel of his mouth against hers. It was dizzying and consuming. She could have stayed like that all night, though in the back of her mind a tiny voice was still trying to remind her that it wasn't real.

For a moment, she felt as if there were fireworks going off in her mind, but when Conrad drew back and whispered, "Thanks" she realized it had just been the flash of the cameras.

"No problem," she said unsteadily.

He led her out the door to the waiting limo and ushered her in. Once they were seated in the quiet space and the car began to move, he said to her, "Tomorrow there will probably be a couple of fairy-tale speculations in the local papers. With any luck, that will turn some attention to the ball on Saturday night."

Lily swallowed, still disconcerted by the kiss. "It seems like there must be an easier way."

He laughed. "What could be easier than this? Stir up a little gossip, have a few pictures in the gossip magazines…" He snapped his fingers. "Done."

She realized it was true. While, on the surface, this plan might seem silly or unnecessary, it was the simplest and most realistic way for Conrad to garner attention. He knew that from a lifetime of being a bachelor prince. The only reason she was having a hard time with it was because she wasn't a very good actress. She couldn't pretend to have feelings for someone when she didn't.

And even more than that, she couldn't pretend *not* to have feelings for someone when she *did*.

"I'm glad it worked out," she said.

Conrad frowned. "What's wrong, then?"

"What makes you think something's wrong?"

"It's obvious. You're…subdued."

It figured that the first guy she'd met who was actually perceptive about her feelings was not only a prince, which put him far out of reach as it was, but was also about to go back home, thousands of miles away. "I'm just tired," she said to him, with what she hoped was a convincing smile. "I don't usually stay up this late."

"Ah." He nodded, but the way he looked at her said he wasn't quite convinced.

They traveled the rest of the way back to the hotel in companionable silence. As Conrad looked out the window, Lily studied his profile. He was so handsome it was almost hard to believe he was real. His features were straight and even. His body was lean but strong. She knew already what it felt like to be in his arms, and as she looked at him now, she felt a crazy sense of longing that she knew could never be fulfilled.

This was bad news, she realized with a sense of dread. She was actually beginning to fall for this guy. A prince. Who had made it absolutely one hundred percent clear that he didn't want any sort of romantic entanglements. Who had, in fact, gone so far as to ask her to help him with this because he *knew* she'd understand that he didn't want a relationship.

Talk about unavailable!

Suddenly Lily couldn't wait until this week was over so she could go back to her normal life.

Chapter Eleven

When Saturday finally arrived, no one would allow Lily to do any work at all.

"It's your day," Karen said, expressing the sentiments of all of Lily's coworkers. "We want you to be pampered so you're well rested for your big night as Cinderella. Don't forget, the rest of us want to hear a really good story from this."

Lily smiled at her friend, knowing it was useless. They wanted a Cinderella story and there was no way they were going to let this be an ordinary day for Lily even though she, herself, wanted nothing more than to distract herself with work.

The local newspapers were filled with glowing accounts of Conrad's acceptance of his father's UN award. The photos were good, too, Lily couldn't help but notice. He looked dashing and handsome, and everything a fairy tale prince could be. The *Times* called him "eloquent," the *Post* called him "a hunk," and Caroline Horton called him, "Lady Penelope's future husband."

Lily had to smile at that one. Conrad was *not* going to be happy about that. In recent days, Caroline Horton had been really ratcheting up the implications about Lady Penelope. The *Post,* meanwhile, had spent equal time speculating about Conrad's relationship with Brittany Oliver ("Is it over?") and Lily ("Who's the Mystery Woman who's captured the Playboy Prince's heart?"). Two or three of the papers, plus *People Weekly,* had run a picture of Lily in Conrad's arms at Bell'arrivo. She had lingered over the picture for several minutes, before finally forcing herself to put it away and stop looking at the press coverage altogether.

Her dress was due to be sent over within a couple of hours, Maurice and Freddy were coming at 4:00 p.m., on Conrad's orders to help her get ready, and at six she and Conrad would go to the ball. Then that was it. Her job was finished.

Soon it would be over, she reminded herself.

But instead of feeling relieved, she felt a sense of emptiness.

The delivery boy for Melborn's was running late. He'd gotten lost on the way to the Montclair and had ended up going east when he needed to go west. When he finally got to the hotel, he was terrified the customer would be furious with him for not having gotten there with the dress earlier.

What a relief it was, then, when the large older woman with the tiara had spotted him coming in.

"Is that the delivery for Prince Conrad from Melborn's?" she asked, smiling a smile that didn't quite reach her eyes.

"Yes, ma'am."

"I'll take it," she said.

The boy was uncertain for a moment. It was supposed to go to Prince Conrad, but there were no orders for anyone to sign for it or anything. And if he couldn't trust an old woman in a tiara, who could he trust?

He handed the dress over. "Here you go."

"Thank you so much," the woman said, snapping her fingers. A younger version of herself came waddling over with a puzzled look on her face. "This is the dress for Conrad's date," she said pointedly to the younger woman. "Take it to *his suite*. On the *third floor*."

The younger woman's eyes widened and she nodded, taking the dress.

The delivery boy waited for another moment, but it became clear he wasn't going to get a tip when the older woman said, "Run along now, boy, I'm sure you have better things to do than stand around here and gawk at royalty."

* * *

"The dress isn't here *yet?*" Maurice asked when he joined Lily and Freddy in a vacant room later that afternoon.

"No," Lily said, frowning at her watch. "It really should be here by now."

"I'm getting to the bottom of this," Maurice huffed, taking his cell phone out. He barked into the phone about the delivery of the dress and waited while whomever he was talking to went to check on it. When he finally spoke again, it was to say, "It *was?* When? Who took delivery of it?" He clipped the phone shut and said, "The dress was delivered two and a half hours ago."

"That's impossible," Lily said, going to the phone. "Everyone here is dying to see it. Someone would have let me know it had arrived." She dialed Karen's extension and asked her if the dress had come. Karen said no, not to her knowledge, but promised to check it out and call Lily right back. When she did, she said that no one had seen it, although one of the bellman had seen a kid come in with a large garment bag and hand it off to Princess Drucille.

"Should I ask her if she took the dress by accident?" Karen offered.

Lily had a bad feeling about this. "No, thanks. I'll take care of this myself."

It took some doing to get Freddy and Maurice to wait in the room and let her go to confront Princess

Drucille by herself, but they finally agreed and, with some trepidation, she went down to her suite on the third floor.

The moment Princess Drucille opened the door, Lily knew what the score was. "I believe a dress from Melborn's was delivered to you by accident today," she said, maintaining a casual tone.

"To *me?*" Princess Drucille laid a hand to her ample breast. "I don't know what you're talking about. Even if I did, I wouldn't be able to help you. You see, my stepson may not have any sense when it comes to women, but *I* do. He will be taking Lady Penelope to the ball tonight."

"You're mistaken," Lily said coolly. "And I'm certain you don't want me to ask him to speak with you about the dress."

The older woman's eyes went small and cold. "I'm certain you don't want *me* to talk to the press about certain details of your arrangement with my stepson."

"I've finished the dress, Mother." Lady Ann's voice preceded her as she walked into view holding scissors and blue scraps of material that were clearly recognizable as the remnants of Lily's dress.

Her heart sank.

She didn't have anything else even remotely suitable to wear and with an hour to go, she didn't know how she was going to find something. What Princess Drucille had done was cruel.

Lily left the room wordlessly, and headed back to

tell Freddy and Maurice the bad news. She met them in the hall, as they were on the way down to find her.

"We couldn't let you do it alone," Freddy said, exchanging a quick look with Maurice. "What's wrong?"

"She got the dress," Lily said.

"Where is it?" Maurice wanted to know.

"Cut into about a hundred pieces in her suite, that's where." Lily shuddered at the memory. What a waste. "Her daughter did the work on her orders, I gather."

"So it's…it's unrepairable?" Maurice asked dubiously.

"It wouldn't even cover a Barbie doll sufficiently at this point."

Ironically it was Maurice who burst into tears. "All of our work. This was supposed to be the happiest night of your life, at least so far, and that—that bi—"

"It's okay, Maurice." Lily put an arm around him. "No need to get all worked up." She couldn't believe *she* was having to comfort *him,* but in a way it made her feel better, too. "There must be another solution."

"Sure if you want to look like you just came off the rack," Maurice snorted.

Freddy nodded his agreement. "It's true. If you buy something now, it will look like you just bought it now."

Lily shrugged. It couldn't be helped. "It's better than going naked, or not going at all."

A door down the hall opened and Bernice Dorbrook poked her head out. "What's going on out here?"

"Oh, I'm so sorry if we bothered you, Bernice—"

Lily was interrupted by Maurice, who immediately launched into the story of what had happened and how awful Princess Drucille was.

Bernice was more than ready to agree. "I told Lily I knew her back when she was just Drucille Germorenko and she was as wicked a girl then as you'd ever want to meet."

This catapulted Bernice, Freddy and Maurice into a lively discussion of how nasty Drucille was, how homely her daughter was, and how positively desperate they both were, along with Lady Penelope, to hook Lady Penelope up with Prince Conrad.

"Excuse me," Lily said, holding up her hand. "Much as I agree with a lot of what you're saying, this isn't helping the immediate situation, which is that I'm supposed to go to a charity ball with Conrad in—" she consulted her watch "—forty-five minutes now, and I don't have anything to wear."

"Oh, don't worry about *that*," Bernice said. "Come in, come in, I have *just* the thing. I wore it to the Academy Awards in 1958 when my husband at the time was up for an award for producing. He didn't win." She sighed. "But the dress is just heavenly. A Valentino."

Maurice and Freddy exchanged excited looks and pushed Lily along behind Bernice. They waited in her elaborate sitting room, which was decorated with framed photos of all of her husbands and moments of her life—fishing with Ernest Hemingway; gossiping with Grace Kelly; standing in front of the Berlin Wall while it was dismantled.

After a few minutes, Bernice emerged from the bedroom with a beautiful black column dress.

"Put it on," Bernice urged. "You can use the bedroom. We'll wait out here."

"Okay." Lily took the dress and went into the bedroom with it, hoping against hope it would fit.

Fit it did. As if it had been sewn on her. The dress itself was floor-length, with a sheer train and thin black satin ribbon that served as straps. The material flattered every curve, not apologizing for them but enhancing them, showing off her womanly figure to its best advantage.

When she emerged from the bedroom, three sets of hands clapped against three open mouths.

"You…look…exquisite," Maurice managed at last.

"Enchanting," Freddy agreed.

"Honey, if I'd looked like that in that dress, I would have gone home that night with Cary Grant," Bernice added, but she couldn't disguise the tears in her eyes.

"Thank you," Lily said, feeling the emotion of the moment herself. "All of you. Bernice, I don't know what I would have done if you hadn't opened your door." She sniffed, then straightened up. "But I don't have time for this sniffle-fest, I've got half an hour before Conrad comes to get me. Freddy, work a miracle on my hair, would you?"

"You've got it!"

They all marched back into the room she was using to get ready and a mere twenty minutes later the transformation was complete. She had never felt more beautiful in her life.

By the time Conrad knocked on the door, she was ready to face just about anything.

His pale blue eyes lit up when he saw her. "You look incredible," he said to her, eliciting enthusiastic nods of agreement from Freddy, Maurice and Bernice. "I've never seen a more beautiful woman."

Lily felt her cheeks burn. "That's not true, but thanks for saying it. Are you ready?"

"I think I'd rather sit here and gaze at you all night," Conrad said with a smile.

Lily heard Freddy and Maurice, several feet away, sigh.

She rolled her eyes. "Come on, let's go before I turn into a pumpkin." She started to walk toward him, then stopped. "Oh, no!"

"What's wrong?" Conrad asked.

She lifted the dress to reveal bare feet. "The shoes I had to go with the other dress would look ridiculous with this."

"What size shoe do you wear?" Maurice asked Bernice quickly.

"Six." She looked at Lily hopefully.

Lily shook her head. "Eight. But it's okay. Look, just have the car stop at the Lo-Cost Shoe Mart down the street on the way out."

"Lo-Cost!" Maurice was aghast.

Lily shot him a look. "I only need them for one night and I don't have time to go trouncing through a department store barefoot. It'll be *fine*." She couldn't believe how much she was having to reassure Maurice tonight. "Honestly, you're worrying about this more than I am!"

Conrad escorted her down to the waiting limo, and opened the door for her himself, shooing the driver back to his place.

When Conrad got in, he looked at Lily's bare feet, then at her, and asked, "How about we go to the airport instead and head for Maui?"

She sighed. "Don't mention Maui to a girl from Brooklyn unless you mean it, Your Highness." She laughed. "It's only November and I'm ready to head for warmer weather. Or colder weather. *Something* more interesting than the miserable drizzly wet cold we have here this time of year."

"I would love to take you away from all of this," Conrad said. "Wherever you want to go."

Blood rose in her cheeks. She didn't know if he was serious or not, but the moment was so special that she didn't want to spoil it by asking.

Tonight was a night for fantasy, and they were off to a great start.

Chapter Twelve

She glanced out the window and saw they were approaching the shoe store. "It's right there," she told the driver, and he pulled up smoothly in front of it. "I'll be right back," she said to Conrad.

He reached for his wallet. "At least let me cover this—"

"Forget it." She laughed. "You don't have denominations small enough for this place." She ran in and five minutes later she emerged with cheap but serviceable black strappy shoes. It didn't matter, no one was going to see them anyway.

Conrad looked on approvingly, then told the driver to take them to the ball.

It was the end of November and as they drove

through the crowded city streets, Lily looked out and really appreciated, for the first time, the festive lights and Christmassy atmosphere that was New York City during the holidays.

"Would you join me in a glass of champagne?" Conrad asked.

Normally she would have felt compelled to refuse, and cited her need to keep her wits about her, but tonight was going to be a celebration. "Absolutely," she said.

He poured, then handed her a glass. "To a wonderful night." He held his glass to hers.

She sipped the champagne and allowed herself to enjoy the fizzly feel of the bubbly liquid. This was fun. She didn't always have to be so serious, she told herself. Sometimes she could just let go and have some fun.

Of course, that was a lot easier with someone at her side. Someone who had the same goals and who was working toward them. That's how it had been with Conrad. They had a common goal: to make this evening a success. This, she imagined, was what a successful marriage was like.

She had another sip of champagne and looked at Conrad.

This, she thought, despite the objections of the little voice of self-protection in her head, was what a good husband would be. Present, but not hovering, helpful but not domineering, supportive without being suffocating. And, above all else, appreciative.

Conrad had said so many appreciative things about her over the past few days. She would miss that feeling when he had gone.

And he would be gone tomorrow.

Where had the time gone? In a way, it felt as if she had known him forever. Now that she'd agreed to it, and especially now that she was alone with him, she felt she could have continued this charade forever. But that wasn't the way it was going to be. She had one night. One night to live the fantasy.

The driver pulled the car up in front of the hall where the ball was to take place, and Lily was astonished at the number of photographers who were waiting by the—yes—red carpet.

This time Conrad waited and allowed the driver to open the door, though he gave Lily an embarrassed little smile about it. "It's expected," he explained.

She laughed, and followed his lead as he emerged from the car into the explosion of camera flashes.

For Lily, who was not used to such a display, it was blinding. Fortunately, Conrad had her hand in his and she allowed him to lead her into the ball, despite the fact that she could barely see for all the flash ghosts in her eyes.

"You get used to it," he whispered. "Fortunately, there aren't that many events."

They stopped at the entrance, where Conrad took questions. Lily played her role, standing by his side smiling while he directed virtually every question toward the cause of the evening. He was masterful at the spin, and she had to admire it.

The only time he wasn't consistent with it was when one of the reporters said, "Is this the future Princess of Beloria with you?"

Conrad looked at her and simply said, while looking into her eyes, "She'd make a lovely princess."

Every muscle in Lily's body clenched at that. She had to remind herself, again and again in rapid succession, that this was pretend.

Once inside, amidst the lights, the flowers, the guests—many of whom were luminaries in their various fields—the time flew by. Conrad kept a protective hand on Lily's shoulder as they moved from one group to another, chatting about the cause, the donations and the success of the foundation.

At one point, Conrad stopped and whispered to Lily, "Why are you being so quiet?"

"I'm in awe," she answered honestly. "You're absolutely amazing at this."

He laughed. "I'm not sure *that's* true. Anyway, feel free to speak up." He looked at her and smiled tenderly. "Or not. Whatever you like. I'm proud to have you at my side whatever you do."

Her heart ached at that sentiment, but as the evening wore on and people began to ask her questions, she was able to draw on her considerable experience as a concierge and answer coherently, even though all she could really think about was Conrad.

Around 10:00 p.m. the orchestra began playing, and Conrad said, "That's our cue."

This she hadn't thought of. "Cue?" she asked with dread.

"To dance."

"That's what I was afraid you were going to say." She swallowed. "I can't dance."

He looked at her for a moment, then laughed softly. "You look petrified."

"Because I'm serious. I *really can't dance*."

He touched her cheek and looked into her eyes for a moment before saying, "It's okay. Come with me." He took her hand and led her out onto a terrace overlooking the city skyline.

"Are you cold?" he asked, taking her into his arms.

"Not at all," she said, and it was true. In his arms she was as warm as if it were midsummer.

The door was propped open just enough so they could hear the music. Conrad took her arms and placed them on his shoulder and waist, then said to her, "It's simple. Like this. Front—" he stepped forward, and she followed "—back," he stepped back, and she did likewise. "Side—" to the side "—together." He smiled. "Perfect. Let's go. Front, back, side, together."

And they danced, alone on the terrace, in the chilly November air, with the lights of New York City shining near and far before them.

It was the most romantic evening of Lily's life.

And it wasn't real.

The song ended and Conrad let go of her, clapping softly. "You're a fast learner," he commented. "Ready to go inside?"

The truth was, she would have liked to stay outside for another hour or two, rather than try and dance in front of people, but she knew what was required of her. "Sure," she said.

He took her hand and led her back into the ballroom.

As soon as they emerged, the crowd erupted into applause, light at first, then thunderous as it drew peoples' attention.

Conrad gave a nod to the bandleader and the music started up again. He led Lily onto the dance floor and they danced until a man she didn't recognize broke in. The next hour was like that, Lily and Conrad kept finding their way back to each other, but common protocol allowed for anyone and everyone to simply break in and separate them.

Lily got used to it, and was beginning to look forward to it when one of her coworkers, Sean, showed up at the corner of the crowd. He signaled her urgently.

Alarmed, she went to him. There was no good reason for anyone from the Montclair to show up unless there was a true emergency.

"You have to come now," Sean whispered to Lily. "It's Gerard. It's an emergency."

Lily glanced back at Conrad, who was on the dance floor with an older woman, and she decided she would handle whatever it was and come back before she was missed.

"What's going on?" she asked. "What's wrong?"

"Come with me," Sean said, leading her down the grand staircase. "It won't take long."

Apprehension crossed her breast. "Sean, what's going on? Is something wrong at the hotel?"

He looked right and left, then opened a door. "In here," he said, opening it.

"What *is* it?" Lily asked, stepping forward, but he closed the door behind her before answering.

"I'm sorry," he said on the other side of the door. "If a guest asks for something, we're supposed to provide it, right?"

"Sean." She tried the doorknob. It was locked. "Sean, what are you doing? If a guest asks for what? Open the door!"

"I can't."

"Why not?"

"Because Princess Drucille ordered this." Lily heard him lean up against the door. "I'm sorry, but she offered me a lot of money and I have a family, three kids, to take care of."

"Sean, let me out of here *now* or you're not going to have a job at all."

"Please try and understand, Lily," he implored. "It's not personal."

She felt along the wall for a light switch. There wasn't one. All she could tell was that she was in some sort of tiny storage room. "Sean!" she shouted. "It's not too late to make this right. Just open the door."

"You'll figure it out," he said, but she noticed his voice was getting farther away. "I'm sorry," he repeated once more, but by then it was obvious he was on his way up the stairs again.

Lily sighed and leaned against the door. This wasn't a dungeon, or at least it wasn't intended to be, so it wasn't blocked off in an incredibly clever manner. It was probably just a closet. She looked up, her eyes adjusting slowly to the dim light, and noticed a transom high over the door.

A transom.

If she could locate something to use as a booster here in the dark, she could use it to climb up and over the transom. She felt around in the dark, and came across some sort of hard cardboard box. With some effort, she turned it upside down and stepped on top of it.

It held her weight sufficiently, but it didn't get her close enough to the window over the door. She felt around some more, half-afraid she would touch something alarming, like a sleeping animal or, perhaps worse, a sleeping person. She didn't, though, and eventually she felt her way across a plastic storage box. It was heavy, and she dumped the contents before lifting it over toward the door and putting it on top of the cardboard box she'd already placed there.

It wasn't easy to climb up but, then again, Lily

had some experience with this sort of thing. She'd always been the adventurer back in the days of the Barrie Home and every time a child freaked out and got stuck at the top of the jungle gym, it was Lily who made her way up to save him or her.

So it was now. She hiked her dress up and pulled herself up to the transom, more concerned with taking care of Bernice's dress than with making her own escape.

When it became evident that she couldn't do both successfully, she dropped back into the closet, removed the dress, and climbed back up with the dress in her hand. Somewhere, out there, she realized there was a soft-porn film producer who would have loved to get a load of this.

She was almost halfway through the transom when she heard a voice on the microphone below. "And now, ladies and gentlemen, His Highness, Prince Conrad of Beloria."

The applause was thunderous.

Lily paused. She had to be careful on his behalf, too, she realized. She couldn't shame her date by dropping into a crowd with nothing on but her underwear and shoes.

She proceeded through the transom carefully, listening for every sound, until she was finally free.

Fortunately she was alone when she hit the floor with only her underwear on, but unfortunately, the moment she slipped her dress back on, Princess Drucille appeared.

"Well, aren't you the athletic one?"

"Prince Conrad is *not* going to take kindly to what you've done."

Princess Drucille looked unconcerned. "He'll take even less kindly to you, if you reveal what just happened and force me to reveal this." She reached into her purse and pulled out a tape player. With a smug look on her face, she pressed a button and they both listened as Lily's and Conrad's recorded voices rose over the din of the party upstairs.

"I have a proposal for you," Conrad said.

"A proposal," Lily answered. *"What is it?"*

"Please take a seat for a moment and consider what I'm going to say carefully before you answer."

"You're making me a little nervous, Your Highness."

"I can see that. And I thought you were the sort who never got nervous."

"Normally I don't. So maybe you ought to just tell me what it is you have in mind."

"I need a woman to pretend to be a companion to me this week. Someone the press could speculate about being a, how do you say it, a love interest."

"Are you asking me to find you a…hired escort?"

Princess Drucille snapped the recorder off. "You don't need to hear more, do you?"

"No," Lily said dully.

"Now." Drucille put the player back in her purse. "It would certainly put Conrad in an unflattering light if that recording were to come out."

It certainly would, Lily agreed silently. "How did you manage to bug his suite twice?"

"Your friend Sean came in quite handy," Drucille said smugly. "*Quite* handy."

"Would you really embarrass your stepson like this?" Lily asked. "Taken out of context, that tape sounds terrible."

"It's not so good taken in context, either," Drucille said. "But if you leave now, I'll just put it away and perhaps I'll forget about it."

"And if I don't leave?"

"There is a hungry reporter downstairs, in the person of Ms. Caroline Horton, who would be very eager to hear this tape." Drucille lifted an eyebrow. "The choice is yours. What will it be?"

Conrad came to the microphone and gave a short speech in his father's honor. He was prepared, so the speech part of it was easy, but unfortunately he spent the entire time wondering where his date had gone. He looked out in the crowd for Lily but didn't see her, and the more time passed the more concerned he grew that she might have left.

So he took to the microphone and gave the gracious speech he had planned on giving in his father's honor, and tried to ignore the fact that the only woman he'd cared about in as long as he could remember appeared to have abandoned him altogether.

So forget it, he told himself. That was just more proof that he didn't need a woman in his life. He *cer-*

tainly didn't need anything that was going to interfere with his concentration on more important matters, like the foundation.

He gave his speech to great applause, then stepped off the dais. Drucille approached him immediately with Lady Penelope and another woman she introduced as "the writer, Caroline Horton." He spent several polite moments with each, and when Caroline asked where his date had gone, he said she had gone to the ladies' room to powder her nose.

"She left, you mean?" Ms. Horton asked in astonishment.

"I haven't seen her for *quite* some time," Drucille said, arching an eyebrow over one beady black eye.

Conrad paused over that then decided to leave it alone. There was no point in arguing with the woman. Instead, he decided, he would make a show of having a good time. He would socialize with everyone and make sure the evening was a pleasant one for his guests.

Regardless of how bad he, personally, felt about Lily's disappearance.

It never once occurred to him that there might be some sinister reason behind it.

So when at last he saw Lily emerging from the stairwell, her hair and dress mussed, his first thoughts were not charitable.

He went to her and took her by the arm, leading her quickly out of the spotlight. "Where have you been?"

"I have to go," she said. "This was a mistake."

"But Lily—what are you talking about?"

"This was just a bad idea," she said, clearly trying to hold back tears. "Go back to what you were doing. It's a lot more important than this conversation."

"I'm not sure about that."

"Trust me," she said.

"I do, but—"

She shook her head frantically. "I have to go. But I truly wish you the best of luck with this evening." She lifted her hem and started to hurry away.

"Wait." He grabbed her arm as she started to pass him. "I need you to stay."

"No—" she shook her head "—you don't." She broke free of his grasp and turned to walk away from him.

He could have sworn before she left he saw tears in her eyes.

"Lily, wait!" He ran after her, but she already had a head start from his own foolish hesitation.

She clambered down the steps out front, and he followed her. When she neared the bottom she stumbled and lost a heel. She paused just long enough to take the whole shoe off, throw it, and get into a passing cab.

"Lily!"

Conrad ran after her, calling for her, and eventually for the cab, to stop, but neither heeded his pleas.

In the end all he was left with was the broken shoe and a heart to match.

* * *

Lily took the cab straight back to her apartment in Brooklyn. She didn't care if it cost a hundred dollars tonight, she needed to get home and to feel like herself again. It had been so long since she had.

During the time she'd been locked in the closet, she'd been almost certain Conrad would show up to "rescue" her at any moment. It had never occurred to her that Drucille might have such a diabolical plan.

Lily knew she'd done the right thing, leaving him at the party. If she'd stayed, Princess Drucille could have walked right up to the microphone and played her little tape.

That would have humiliated Conrad and put shame on the whole event.

Conrad hesitated for a moment, torn between the ball he was supposed to be hosting and the woman he was supposed to be escorting. He followed the path she'd taken, picking up the shoe she'd thrown in anger. It didn't take him long to put his priorities in order.

He caught the next cab, took it back to the Montclair and asked the driver to wait outside.

Once in the hotel, he'd asked Andy for Lily's home address. It only took a little persuasion before he relinquished it.

"I'm *such* a fan of romance," he said.

Conrad got back into the cab, the shoe still tightly

grasped in his hand, and gave the driver the Brooklyn address. It seemed to take forever to get there, though Conrad wasn't sure whether that was because of the distance or the time that elapsed since she'd left thinking he didn't care about her.

Whatever else happened, he *had* to let her know he *did* care. He cared an awful lot. He just wasn't used to worrying...that was the difference.

The driver pulled the cab up in front of a small building in Brooklyn. It was only three stories high and there was a maze of fire escapes criss-crossing down the wall. Conrad gave half a thought to the possibility of Lily escaping via the fire escape when she realized that he was at the door, but no matter how angry she was he couldn't believe she'd go that far.

He went to the apartment number Andy had given him and knocked. After a moment, with no answer, he knocked again, adding, "I know you're in there, Lily Tilden. Answer the door."

There followed the sound of a chain scraping across the latch, and she opened the door. "What do you want?" she asked.

He held the broken shoe out to her. "You lost this." The irony of his extending the shoe belonging to the woman he might want to marry was not lost on him.

She looked at it, then at him, and shook her head. "This isn't a fairy tale."

"No kidding." He smiled, wishing she would

respond with a smile of her own. "I don't remember any story in which the prince has to ride through twenty-odd miles of pot holes and traffic to get to his princess."

She winced at the designation. "I'm not a princess."

"Maybe not," he said looking into her eyes deeply, penetratingly. "But you could be."

She closed her eyes for a moment, then said, "I'm tired, Conrad. It's been a long night and I really need to go to sleep."

"What happened?" he asked. "What changed?"

She started to speak, then stopped and shook her head. Finally she just said, "Nothing changed, I guess I'm just exhausted from everything I've had to do this week."

His heart broke at that moment. Broke in a way he had never dreamed it could. Only then did he realize he was in love with Lily.

He gave a single nod. "I'll go, then. But you know where to find me. I'll still be here for another twenty-four hours."

"Then you leave for your own country. Let's say goodbye now. It was fun. Thanks for..." She shrugged. "For everything."

He looked at her for a moment, but had no response. Instead he set the shoe down by her door and said, "No, Lily, thank *you*. I hope we'll meet again someday." He turned to leave.

"Conrad—" she began.

He stopped and turned to face her.

After a hesitation that seemed to last forever, she shook her head and, with pain in her eyes, said, "If I don't see you again, really, thank you. This was an amazing week."

He had no response for that. "You're welcome" would have been patronizing, and "Oh no, thank *you*" would have sounded sarcastic.

So all he could do was give her a brief nod and leave. And he did.

Chapter Thirteen

"So you just let him go, huh?" Rose asked, glancing at her sister in the passenger seat as they drove upstate to finally meet their missing sister. "So long, thanks for stopping by."

"It wasn't that easy," Lily objected. "But I had to do it. His wicked stepmother was standing by with her tape recorder."

"But you know you two could concoct a response to that in ten minutes. What's the *real* reason you haven't spoken to him again?"

Lily sniffed. "We're from two different worlds. We didn't have a chance together."

"Why not?" Rose wanted to know. "If Warren and I can make it, you and Conrad certainly can."

Lily shook her head. "Warren's one of us, really. He comes from where we come from. He's certainly built himself a mighty empire, but he did it by hand, not by hundreds of years of conquering and ruling."

"You make it sound like Conrad did it all himself. That was his family. His *heritage*. The very thing we're trying to find for ourselves right now. Why damn him for it?"

Lily put a hand to her eyes and turned toward the window. It seemed she was always close to tears these days. Lily Tilden, who had spent a lifetime being known as "the fearless one," was now an emotional wreck. It was crazy.

"I don't damn him for it," she said. "I just can't be *with* him."

"But why not?"

"Well, for one thing, Rose, because he doesn't want me. Now can we please drop the subject? I think this is our exit." She looked at the map on her lap and said, "Yes, exit one-seventy-three, this is it."

Rose eased the car onto the exit and followed Lily's directions to the home of Laurel Standish, their long-lost sister. As they got closer, both sisters began to feel apprehensive.

After what seemed like ages, Rose pulled the car into the driveway of the small brown cabin-style home and turned the ignition off. "Are you ready?" she asked.

"As ready as I'll ever be," Lily said with a sigh. "How about you?"

"Ditto."

They got out of the car and reached for each other's hands as they walked to the front door of the cabin. It took about ten minutes of knocking before an old man finally made his way to the front door and worked the latch open. "Yes?"

"Hi," Lily said, a bit awkwardly. "We're looking for Laurel Standish. We were told she lives here."

"You're too late," the old man said, blinking hard and going to shut the door.

Rose stopped him. "Wait. What do you mean we're too late? Does Laurel live here?"

"Did once," he said, shaking his head. "But she's gone now."

A terrible feeling lodged in the pit of Lily's stomach. She swallowed hard. "What do you mean *gone?*"

The man looked from Lily to Rose and back, then said, "She died in a plane crash two weeks ago."

Lily felt like she'd been punched in the stomach. Died? *Died?* They'd come this close to finding the sister they'd never even known they had, only to find that she had died just two weeks ago?

It was so unfair she couldn't believe it was true.

Rose found her voice first. "I'm…I'm so sorry to hear that. So sorry." Her voice cracked but she continued, "We've just learned that Laurel might have been our sister."

For the first time since they'd come to the door, the old man's facial expression softened. "Are you Lily and Rose?"

The sisters exchanged looks of shock.

"Yes," Lily said to him. "How did you know?"

"I'm Bart Standish, Laurel's father." There was a long pause before he said, "We knew about you, my wife and myself. Saw you at the orphanage when we took Laurel home. We just—" he shook his head "—we couldn't afford to take you all."

Rose bit her trembling lip.

Lily spoke instead. "It's okay, we understand that. Did…did Laurel know about us?"

He shook his head. "My wife didn't want her to know. She didn't even want her to know she was adopted, so we kept it from her all these years. Then my wife passed and…" He stepped back and opened the door. "Maybe you ought to come in."

He led the sisters to a modest den and offered them seats on a threadbare sofa. Then he asked them to wait for a moment while he left the room. He was back only a few minutes later, with a small photo album and a book. He handed them to Lily and Rose. "I guess these belong to you now."

"What are they?" Rose asked.

But Lily, who opened the photo album, could tell right away. "These are our parents," she said quietly. "Look." She held the little book out for Rose to see.

And there they were, two people who were a perfect mix of Rose and Lily's features. Their father had Rose's straight brow, their mother had the same quirk of the lips that Lily did. It was like looking at their own genetic fingerprints.

"They were left at the Barrie Home along with you girls," the old man said in answer to Rose and Lily's unasked questions. "Laurel only got them a couple of years ago and she took them with her overseas, but when the plane crashed…well, they sent back whatever was left from the last place she'd stayed."

Rose opened the book and Lily looked over her shoulder. Most of the pages were blank but it opened with a letter to "Rose, Lily and Laurel." Lily fought a feeling of anger that she and Rose had spent all these years having to guess at who they were without the benefit of these roadmaps that had, obviously, been left for them.

"What does it say?" she asked Rose.

"You'll want to take the book along with you, and you should. It's a letter to you from your mother, explaining that your father passed away in an accident when you were just over a year old. She wasn't able to care for you herself, and so she left you in the church of St. James, and watched until Sister Gladys came along and found you and took you all back to the orphanage. Apparently she left the photos and the diary for you after she knew you were safely in the home."

Lily was overcome by emotion. "But why didn't anyone tell us this? After all these years, why didn't *someone* let us know *something* of our heritage?" She looked from Rose to the old man.

Rose didn't have an answer, but Bart Standish

simply said, "I'm sorry now that we never told Laurel about her sisters."

"So she didn't know about us at all?" Rose asked. "You didn't tell her anything?"

"Only the truth as we knew it. That her mother lost her father and couldn't take care of her." He was curiously dry-eyed at this revelation, though he was mercifully forthcoming with what details he did have.

Lily handed Rose both books and said to the old man, "Is there anything else you can tell us about our sister?"

He paused for a moment, then shook his head. "I don't know anything. She was good at sports. Always took care of the neighborhood kids and animals. That's really all I know. I spent so much time away, working, that I barely recognized Laurel *or* her mother when I came home. I'm sorry. Sorrier than you can imagine. You take those books now. I have no use for them." He headed toward the door and opened it. "I'm tired now. I hope you understand."

Lily was the first to stand. "Thank you so much for your time and for those books. They mean more than you could imagine."

He nodded and held the door open while Lily and Rose passed by. "Good luck to you two," he said. "I hope you get everything you want out of life."

Lily and Rose looked at each other, then went to the car. They heard the front door close before they had taken the final step off the porch.

"What do you make of that?" Rose asked, putting her hands on the steering wheel and turning to look at Lily.

"I think our sister left us a great blessing," Lily said, patting the books. "We finally know something of where we came from. And we know that we were wanted. Listen to this—" She opened the diary and read from it. "'My sweet girls, if I had any other option, I would take it but I cannot love you as much as I do and allow you to live the life of hardship and struggle you would have if I had to raise you alone. It is only because I love you so much that I give you up. Please forgive me.'"

Lily closed the book and looked at Rose with teary eyes. "I was always a little afraid that we'd been left because we weren't wanted. Now we know that's not true."

Rose nodded and started the car, backing slowly out of the lot and out of the environment that had almost completed their triumvirate.

She stopped, suddenly, when Laurel's father came out of the house, waving his hands. He came to the passenger door and Lily lowered the window.

"You should have these, too," he said, thrusting a manila envelope into Lily's hands. "They're Laurel's letters from overseas. Maybe they'll help you get to know your sister some. The one on top is the last one she sent. You should read it."

He didn't leave them any time even to thank him, just turned on his heels and went back into the house, the typical, salty old New Englander.

"So read the letter," Rose said.

Lily opened the envelope and found the top letter. The envelope was postmarked just over two weeks prior.

"'Dad,'" Lily read, "'things are volatile here. I wanted to write and let you know that I will continue to send money to help you with the house payments. If anything should happen to me, I have a friend here named Glenna Cunliffe, who has promised to see to it that you get my pay and my belongings. In the event that something happens, she will be in touch with you—'" Lily stopped and looked at her sister.

Rose's face was pale, and her hands where tight on the steering wheel. "Pretty prophetic, huh?"

"Eerily so." Lily looked back at the letter in her hand. "She signed it after that. There are only a couple of other letters and postcards in here." She opened a letter, then folded it and put it back. "Very brief. It seems like Laurel wasn't that close to her parents. At least not to her father."

"That's sad."

Lily nodded and put the letter back in the manila envelope. "We should look for this Glenna Cunliffe. Maybe she can tell us more about Laurel."

"I'll ask George Smith to check her out and let us know when she's back in the States."

Lily sighed and leaned back against her seat. "Still, this is incredible. Laurel may be gone, but she's left us a great gift." She gestured toward the photo album and the diary and wiped the tears off her cheeks. "We finally have some sense of where we came from."

Rose nodded. "It's funny, it feels like the answer to a riddle I've been trying to figure out for years."

"Or just a question," Lily commented. "Are you worth it? Were you wanted?" She ran her hand over the cover of the diary. "Knowing that makes a huge difference."

"It does. But maybe it shouldn't. I mean, we should have known all along we were worthy of love, regardless of how we ended up at the Barrie Home."

Lily looked at her sister and reached over to pat her shoulder. "But you always wondered, didn't you? I did."

Rose glanced at Lily. "Yes. And if Warren hadn't come along when he did, and persisted the way he did, I'm not sure I ever would have believed I was worthy of a loving relationship." She swiped a tear off her cheek. "But I could have told you *you* were. In fact, I think I *did*."

"Many times," Lily said, looking out the window at the passing scenery. Suddenly everything looked different. It was as if this small new understanding of her family had given her a huge new understanding of the world. "You know, it's easy to say that Laurel is a missing piece that we can never get back, but she still filled a void."

Rose nodded. "And she provided a reminder that

family is what you make it, not just where your blood matches." She glanced at Lily. "It doesn't matter where you come from, it's where you end up that counts."

Lily narrowed her eyes at her sister, realizing she was making reference to Prince Conrad. "He's leaving today so you can't talk me into going to him."

Rose shrugged. "You're even more stubborn than I am."

"Maybe I'm just more realistic," Lily offered. "Ever think of that?"

Rose snorted and drove the car onto the highway.

An hour and a half later, as they were driving over the George Washington Bridge into the city, Lily's cell phone rang.

It was Karen. "Are you watching Channel Eight?"

Channel Eight was the local cable news network. "No, I'm in the car. Why?"

"Get to the hotel right away," Karen said. "Double park. Triple park if you have to. Prince Conrad is about to give a press conference. Reporters are asking about you."

Lily hung up the phone, frowning, and told Rose what Karen had said.

"We're five minutes away," Rose pointed out. "I'll pull up to the front and let you out, then I'll park and meet you inside."

"I'm a little nervous," Lily confessed.

Rose looked at her. "Since when do you get nervous?"

"Since I fell in love with a prince," Lily said.

"So you admit it! You're in love with him!"

"Yes, I'm in love with him. So?"

Rose smiled and gunned the engine. "So we need to get you to him before he leaves."

"But—"

"But nothing. I'm not letting you miss out on the best thing that ever happened to you just because you're too stubborn to admit it."

Chapter Fourteen

By the time Lily got into the conference room, Conrad had evidently finished speaking and was taking the last of the questions.

Caroline Horton was there, along with several other New York gossip luminaries. Princess Drucille sat directly up front, flanked by her daughter, Lady Ann, and Lady Penelope.

A reporter raised his hand and Conrad lowered a blue gaze on him and nodded.

"The American woman you took to the charity ball last night," the man said. "Who was she?"

"Her name was Lily Tilden," Conrad said slowly, then pointed to another questioner.

"Is she the next Princess of Beloria?"

"That would be my fondest wish." Conrad said. "But—" His gaze landed on Lily and he stopped speaking.

"But what, Your Highness?"

"But I don't know if she'll have me," he said evenly. "You see, Miss Tilden has been through quite a lot because of me. My late father's wife tried to blackmail her into staying away from me." He smiled, without a hint of humor. "Only a woman desperate to hold on to a lifestyle she knows she does not deserve would go to such lengths."

"What did she try to blackmail her with?" someone in the crowd asked.

Conrad paused. "A recording of myself asking Miss Tilden to accompany me tonight. She, quite prudently, was hesitant to become involved with me. Nevertheless, I tried to win her over." He caught Lily's eye. "I hope I won her over."

Lily nodded, trembling inside.

"Because if I did, and if she'd agree to be my wife, I would be the luckiest man on the face of the earth."

Hands shot up all around them but Conrad only had eyes for Lily.

"Does that mean you'll get married?" someone asked.

"I don't know." Conrad raised an eyebrow at Lily. "Does it?"

She swallowed hard.

He extended a hand toward her and suddenly everyone around her realized who she was.

"It's her!"

"What about it, Miss Tilden, will you marry Prince Conrad?"

She pressed her lips together to keep from crying, and walked carefully toward Conrad, ignoring the questions and flashbulbs that were shooting around her. She had her eyes and her mind set on only one thing: Conrad.

And he, in turn, appeared to have only her in mind. He took her hand as soon as she was close enough, and helped her up to join him.

"What do you say, Miss Tilden?" he said quietly, then got down on one knee before her. "Will you marry me?"

For the first time in her life, Lily felt as if she knew where she belonged. She felt whole in a way that she never had before. She felt *at home* in a way she never had before.

The certainty that this was what she wanted swelled like a great wave inside her. She'd never been so sure of anything in her life.

Words failed her, she could only nod.

"It's a yes!" someone yelled.

The word *yes* bounced around the room like an echo.

Conrad stood up and pulled Lily into his arms. "Are you sure?" he asked quietly in her ear. "I don't want you to feel pressured because of the crowd."

"Crowd?" she repeated. "What crowd?"

He laughed and kissed her lips, then turned to the

reporters. "I didn't plan this, but it looks like you got the story you were asking for all week. Beloria has a new princess and her name is Lily." He smiled at his new fiancée and squeezed her hand, sending a thrill through to her fingertips. "And she's made me the happiest man alive."

Epilogue

"Can I look yet?"

"One more moment."

"Conrad, I've had this blindfold on since we took the helicopter from the airport. It's starting to itch."

Conrad laughed. "It's only been twenty minutes."

She smiled. "Then let me put it on you for twenty minutes and see how you like it."

She felt him swoop close to her ear, and he whispered, "Tonight. That sounds like a very interesting idea."

Lily's skin tingled at his sultry tone, and at the promise of spending tonight with him in bed. And tomorrow night. And the night after that. And so on, forever.

Her thoughts were just getting vivid, when Conrad reached over and pulled the blindfold off.

The first thing she saw was him, in all his handsome, princely glory. He smiled and, holding her gaze, swooped her into his arms, like the heroine of an old movie. "Princess Lily, welcome home."

Only then did she look up and see the magnificent white castle before them. It was tall and majestic, with arched lead windows, and winding spires that reached into the endless blue sky above. Walt Disney himself couldn't have come up with a more romantic fairy tale castle.

She could hardly believe it was real.

"You're not saying we're going to live here, are you?"

Conrad laughed. "Of course. What else would we do with it?"

Her wide-eyed gaze traveled over the bleached white stone. "Turn it into a museum?" She looked back at Conrad. "I never dreamed I'd live someplace as beautiful as this."

"Wait until you see the inside. But first I must carry you over the threshold myself. That is the American tradition, isn't it?"

Lily nodded. "I think it's supposed to bring good luck."

Conrad carried her into a great marble hall and set her down, keeping his arms around her waist. "We don't need luck," he said to her, drawing her close against him. "We have destiny on our side."

Her breath caught in her throat. It was such a romantic notion, yet it was exactly what she felt herself. "Do you really believe that?"

He nodded. "I knew the moment I first saw you that fate had brought me to you. And now—" he nodded toward the staircase "—fate has brought you home to me. Let's go to our bedroom, Princess. I'll give you a tour later. For now…" He kissed her, slow and deep, then whispered in her ear, "Now I need to show you how much I treasure you."

* * * * *

*Don't miss Laurel's story, coming
to Harlequin Romance in 2007.*

**Hidden in the secrets of antiquity,
lies the unimagined truth...**

Introducing

a brand-new line filled with mystery
and suspense, action and adventure,
and a fascinating look into history.

And it all begins with DESTINY.

In a sealed crypt in
France, where the
terrifying legend of
the beast of Gevaudan
begins to unravel,
Annja Creed discovers
a stunning artifact
that will seal her destiny.

*Available every other
month starting
July 2006, wherever
you buy books.*

GRA1

If you enjoyed what you just read,
then we've got an offer you can't resist!

Take 2 bestselling
love stories FREE!
Plus get a FREE surprise gift!

Page-turning drama…

Exotic, glamorous locations…

Intense emotion and passionate seduction…

Sheikhs, princes and billionaire tycoons…

This summer, may we suggest:

THE SHEIKH'S DISOBEDIENT BRIDE
by Jane Porter

On sale June.

AT THE GREEK TYCOON'S BIDDING
by Cathy Williams

On sale July.

THE ITALIAN MILLIONAIRE'S VIRGIN WIFE

On sale August.

With new titles to choose from every month, discover a world of romance in our books written by internationally bestselling authors.

HARLEQUIN® *Presents*

It's the ultimate in quality romance!

Available wherever Harlequin books are sold.

www.eHarlequin.com

HPGEN06

This riveting new saga begins with

In the Dark

by national bestselling author

JUDITH ARNOLD

The party at Hotel Marchand is in full swing when the lights suddenly go out. What does head of security Mac Jensen do first? He's torn between two jobs—protecting the guests at the hotel and keeping the woman he loves safe.

A woman to protect. A hotel to secure. And no idea who's determined to harm them.

On Sale June 2006

SILHOUETTE *Romance*

A family saga begins to unravel
when the doors to the Bella Lucia
Restaurant Empire are opened...

The Brides of Bella Lucia

*A family torn apart by secrets,
reunited by marriage*

AUGUST 2006

COMING HOME TO THE COWBOY
by Patricia Thayer

Find out what happens to Rebecca Valentine when
her relationship with a millionaire cowboy and single
dad moves from professional to personal.

SEPTEMBER 2006

The Valentine family saga continues in

HARLEQUIN *Romance*

with **THE REBEL PRINCE** by Raye Morgan

SRBB0706

Silhouette® BOMBSHELL™

The Marian priestesses were destroyed long ago, but their daughters live on. The time has come for the heiresses to learn of their legacy, to unite the pieces of a powerful mosaic and bring light to a secret their ancestors died to protect.

The Madonna Key

Follow their quests each month.

SILHOUETTE *Romance*®

COMING NEXT MONTH

#1822 PRICELESS GIFTS—Cara Colter
A Father's Wish

Sure her father is trying to keep her safe from some crazed stalker, but firing her staff and removing her from her luxury suite to her crazy aunt's farm is going too far! Chelsea King is pretty sure the situation can't get any worse—until she meets her new bodyguard, Randall Peabody. An ex-soldier—broken, scarred, protective— Randall stirs something in Chelsea and makes her feel as if she hasn't really lived until now....

#1823 THE BRIDE'S BEST MAN—Judy Christenberry

Logic and order are Shelby Cook's typical, lawyerly methods. But when she goes with her aunt on a much-needed vacation to Hawaii, she never expects to meet her long-lost father and to be attracted to his friend Pete Campbell. Shelby doesn't think the attraction will go anywhere, but Pete is about to show her that true love defies all limitations and logic!

#1824 ONE MAN AND A BABY—Susan Meier
The Cupid Campaign

Experience has taught Ashley Meljac not to trust her instincts regarding men, especially when it comes to the town's resident bad boy—Rick Capriotti. Still, something in the way he cares for his baby makes her forget the past and dream about a future with him and his adorable toddler....

#1825 HERE WITH ME—Holly Jacobs

After divorce and a miscarriage, Lee Singer just craves quiet and solitude. But soon Adam Benton, a workaholic with a one-year-old in tow, arrives back in town. And all too soon he's brought noise and life to her world and got her questioning what she truly desires.